Maggie's Treasure

GATLIN FIELDS

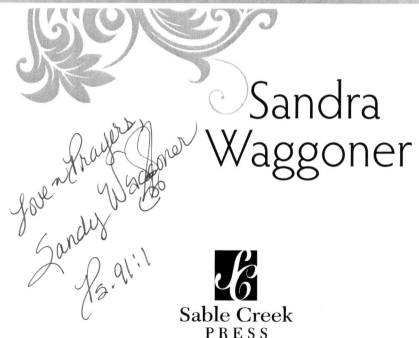

Sandra Waggoner

Love n Prayers
Sandy Waggoner
Ps. 91:1

Sable Creek
PRESS

First printing 2005
Second printing 2008

Cover and text design by Diane King, www.dkingdesigner.com
Cover photo of barn © 2008 istockphoto.com/Tracy Tucker
Back cover photo © 2008 istockphoto.com/Jill Fromer

Scripture taken from the King James Version. Public domain.

Published by Sable Creek Press, PO Box 12217, Glendale, Arizona 85318
www.sablecreekpress.com

Publisher's Cataloging-in-Publication data

Waggoner, Sandra.
    Maggie's treasure / Sandra Waggoner.
        p. cm.   "Gatlin Fields, Book One"
    ISBN 978-0-976-68230-1
    Summary: When an unwanted family, a cruel busybody and a deadly explosion bring young Maggie to despair, she learns about God and reveals her secret.
    1. Depressions--1929--Kansas--Juvenile fiction. 2. Family life--Kansas--Fiction. 3. Stepmothers--Juvenile fiction. 4. Fathers and daughters--Juvenile fiction. 5. Christian fiction. I. Title.

PZ7.W124135 .Ma 2008
[Fic]--dc22
                                                            2007942817

Printed in the United States of America.

Especially for Mom and Dad,
who taught me the worth of work;
Greg, who encouraged me to work;
and Janet, who made it work.

Romans 8:28
"And we know that all things work together for good to them that love God, to them that are the called according to his purpose."

Chapters

1 We Do 7

2 Boxcar 13

3 Company 21

4 Snow Feathers 29

5 Ask the Stars 36

6 The God in Your Heart 43

7 Opal Trouble 50

8 Gone 60

9 Mustard Seeds 67

10 This Stinks! 75

11 With This Ring 83

CHAPTER 1

We Do

A thin film of dust covered the inside of the church. Maggie eased forward. Ever so gently her finger penned her name on the dusty pew in front of her. Thump! Maggie swallowed, leaned back, and rubbed her head where her father had gently but completely gotten her attention.

"Quit playin' and pay attention to the preacher," he whispered into her ear.

Maggie straightened her dress. Well, it wasn't *exactly* hers. It had been three years since she'd worn anything but overalls, and now she was eleven and she'd done a lot of growing in that time. This dress was Mama's, but Daddy had insisted she wear it. "After all, you're meetin' your new mama and new sisters for the first time," he had explained with a smile.

Maggie studied the dress. It was old, but there had been no money to buy a new one. There had been no money for anything. Daddy had pulled out Mama's dresser drawer, carried it into Maggie and placed it in her arms. Then he had choked over a few words, telling her to see if she could find anything suitable for church. She remembered how his shoulders had drooped when he'd turned and quietly walked to the barn. That's when Maggie had found the dress. It still smelled like Mama. Daddy had wanted her to wash it, but Maggie had hung it on the clothesline to air. She didn't want to lose the aroma that flooded her heart with memories. She could still remember Mama wearing that dress.

Tiny pink rosebuds spattered the creamy material and there was a touch of lace about the collar. Mama had laughed in that dress and teased Daddy about her being a grand refined woman whenever she wore it. She had looked beautiful in it. It didn't look the same on Maggie. She had rolled up the waist several times and cinched it with an old leather belt. The belt didn't show though, because the top of the dress bloused over it. She would have to be sure to keep the tail of the belt tucked in so it didn't flop down and look out of place. She found a safety pin to modestly close the drooping collar.

Maggie smashed her eyes shut. Although it had been three years, many memories still made her want to cry. She clenched her fists and shoved them into the dress pockets. Her hand landed on cold metal—Mama's compact! Maggie had found it with a bunch of other treasures in Mama's drawer. In fact, Maggie had dumped every single thing in Mama's drawer into the bottom of her carpetbag. She wanted all she could bring of Mama with her when she went to this new place Daddy had promised her. She pulled the compact from her pocket and opened it. A mirror was a priceless possession and she would treasure it forever, even if it was broken. She would have to be careful with it. Maggie gazed into her own face for only a few moments. After all, she knew what she looked like. Her eyes were sometimes blue and sometimes green, but nothing special. Her hair was what Mama had called dishwater blonde, which meant dirty blonde. Freckles splashed across her nose. Maggie smiled as she remembered Mama had always teased her that her freckles were angel spit. Daddy would scoop Maggie into his arms, twirl her high in the air and assure her they were really angel kisses!

Maggie quickly looked up at the preacher. She didn't want to see her memories anymore. Before she could clamp the compact shut the mirror caught movement overhead. Maggie paused, a smile spreading across her face invited her eyes to dance. A squirrel scampered in the rafters, clutching something tightly in his mouth. Maggie squinted to study the intruder.

"Amen and amen!" Pastor Olson bellowed and pounded the pulpit. Maggie's eyes flew wide as the squirrel dropped its cargo. In slow motion it sailed through the air and bombed a sleeping man on the top of his bald head. He snorted and blurted out, "Dinner ready yet?"

Like a summer thunderstorm, laughter rippled through the little wooden church.

"Arnold! Be quiet!" Embarrassed, the man's wife jabbed him in the ribs. Her hush settled the whole congregation.

Pastor Olson cleared his throat and stifled the smile that played at the corners of his mustache. It was clear that any serious thought was gone. "Let's bow our heads and pray. Our Father, we thank you for your promise of victory to overcome whatever trials we may face in this life. We pray for your blessing of badly needed rain upon this land you have given us.

Lord, you know we need it something awful. Please, Father, bless each of us as we go our separate ways," he paused, "and please bless Arnold's dinner."

Maggie peeked up at the preacher. She liked him because he wasn't mad at Arnold for spoiling his sermon. Pastor Olson tipped his head at Arnold who now sat with a sheepish look on his face. Arnold's wife jabbed him in the ribs again. Arnold dropped his head. As the preacher scanned the congregation, he caught Maggie's eye and winked. Quickly she closed her eyes.

"Amen."

Before Pastor Olson could dismiss the people, Maggie heard a rustle beside her as Daddy stood. He took a long, deep breath and rolled his hat over and over in his big calloused hands. "Sir . . . uh . . . brother . . . uh . . . preacher . . ."

"Yes?" Pastor Olson said.

"We was a wonderin' . . . uh . . . Sue and me . . . if you could take a minute to hitch us?" Daddy's voice dwindled to a whisper.

Gasps of surprise surrounded the couple and excitement filled the little church building.

Maggie's heart stopped. How had this happened anyway? She had never even met this Sue until they drove into town this morning. Daddy had explained she was an old friend of the family, they had been writing, and that Maggie needed a mama. That was supposed to explain everything, but Maggie didn't understand any of it.

The preacher paused only for a moment. His gentle smile comforted Maggie's daddy. "Well . . . Sir . . . Mr. . . . "

"Daniels. Sam Daniels," Daddy filled in the blank.

"Mr. Daniels, do you have a license?"

"Yes, sir." Daddy fumbled in his pocket and pulled out a piece of folded paper. The preacher met him in the aisle and studied the document. He lifted his head and let his eyes settle on Sue. "Sue, is this the gentleman you have talked with me about?" The eyes of the whole church turned to Sue. She nodded.

"The papers look good, Mr. Daniels." Pastor Olson turned to the people. "Anyone object to taking a few minutes for a wedding?"

Chuckles and cheers rose all around amid tidbits of conversation.

"Well, I never!"

"Who would have thought it!"

"How in the world did Sue keep this a secret from me?"

"Come on up to the front." The preacher motioned them to follow as he walked back to the pulpit.

Sam took Sue's arm, then turned to Maggie and grabbed her hand. "Come on Maggie, I want you to be part of this ceremony."

Maggie swallowed. She was in a new place with new people and she didn't want to be here. She looked to where her new mama and new sisters stood waiting. She didn't want a new family. She wanted to run. She wanted to shout, "No! Stop! Don't!" Her whole being trembled.

Sam let go of Sue's arm and knelt beside Maggie. He spoke quietly, "Honey, I will always love your mama. I see her everyday in you. I swear she lives and walks in you, but honey, she is not here." He swallowed a lump in his throat. "She would want me to take the best care of you I can, and this is it. Sue is an awfully nice lady and she can teach you to be one. I can't Maggie. I can't do that, but I can give you someone who can. Please, Maggie, trust me?"

Bravely Maggie stood. "Okay, Daddy," she whispered. She slipped her hand into his big one and together they walked up the aisle.

Sam and Sue exchanged their vows. Afterwards people hugged and congratulated the newlyweds. Maggie didn't remember much of what happened, except that she never let go of her daddy's hand.

Boxcar

T
he doors of the little church swung shut behind the new family. Maggie stood on the wooden porch and knew those doors had slammed as well on the life she had known. She shook more with each step she took.

A tall, thin woman who smelled like drugstore perfume hugged Sue and scolded, "If I had known about this here wedding, Sue, I would have brought a handful of rice to throw at the two of you. It's supposed to bring you good luck and we all could sure use some good luck these days."

Sue smiled. "It's all right, Mrs. Crenshaw. I reckon you'd best not be wasting your rice on us. Just say a prayer. More good will come of that than the rice."

Maggie looked up at Sue. She looked nice. But so did their old, cantankerous cow, Lulubelle. You just had to learn to stay away from her backside and never offer your backside to her. Lulubelle could take a hunk of hide quick as a wink and do it almost with a smile. Maggie didn't know how many times Daddy had whacked Lulubelle for that and he still called her a good ol' girl.

Most of the people had now gathered in the street outside the church to cheer the newlyweds. Sam guided Sue through them and their best wishes to the old buckboard. Gently he helped his new wife onto the seat of the wagon. Then he turned to the girls. Opal giggled as Mr. Daniels tossed her over the side into the hay. Maggie's heart lurched. She turned her back, climbing up the wheel and over the side of the wagon on her own. As she settled deep into the hay, Opal's younger sister, Ruby, landed beside Opal. Ruby clapped her hands and giggled, "Oh, I like having a daddy!"

Maggie's heart felt ripped open. That was *her* daddy. Was he going to be *their* daddy now? She stared at them from the opposite side of the wagon. Maggie figured Opal must be about eight because she had big, new front teeth. Her thick, curly hair was almost black. She had Lulubelle eyelashes that surrounded her baby blue eyes and it looked like the angels had done a little spitting on her nose, too. Ruby was probably five. All her teeth were still baby teeth. She had the same kind of curly black hair Opal had and the same baby blues, but the angels had missed her.

The wagon pulled slowly out into traffic. Ben and Maude kept moving their ears in circles. They were good horses, but they were skittish around automobiles. The street was quiet, but the animals could still pick up the scent of gasoline exhaust. Tied to the back of the wagon, Lulubelle bellowed her objection as she was pulled along.

"Which way, Sue? It's been years since I've been here, and boy how things have changed!" Sam said.

"Remember the old Gatlin mansion?"

Sam nodded.

"We're across the alley behind it. It's really my first husband's old pasture, but it has been in Albert's family for the past thirty years. Mr. Thomas Gatlin would like to get his hands on it, but I'm not of a mind to sell. He's offered a pretty penny and there have been times I've been tempted, but I didn't know where I'd go or what I'd do. Besides, Albert refused to sell to him, so I just never felt comfortable with the idea," Sue explained.

"Oh," Sam paused, then raised his eyebrows. "You live in the ritzy neighborhood?"

"Wait until you see it," she warned. "I'm so afraid you'll be disappointed."

"We're just country folk, Sue. City living will take some getting used to, but we aren't gonna be disappointed with what we live in." He paused, "Is it an apartment?"

"No, and this isn't a city," she laughed. "It's only a town."

"There are automobiles. That makes it a city." As if to add to his case, a passing automobile beeped. Ben reared and Maude tried to take to the sidewalk. "Whoa! Ben, Maude! Whoa, now!" Sam spoke with authority.

Wide eyed, Opal and Ruby clung to the side of the wagon and began screaming.

"Hush! Girls, hush!" Sue ordered.

Maggie blinked. "It's okay," she reassured her new sisters. "Ben and Maude will listen to Daddy, but if you do a bunch of yelling like you're doing, that'll scare them and they won't be able to hear his voice. If they get too scared, they're likely to run away."

"Run away?" Opal shrieked.

Ruby started howling.

"They won't run away if you're quiet." Maggie smashed her finger to her lips to emphasize her words.

Opal understood. She slapped her hand over Ruby's mouth. "Hush it up," she warned.

"Easy now, Ben. That's better, Maude. Easy does it," Daddy soothed. The horses calmed down and so did everyone in the wagon. Opal and Ruby looked like they were afraid to breathe, much less talk. That was okay with Maggie. She watched downtown pass by and began scanning houses. One of these was sure to be their destination. House after house faded into the background as the wagon rolled on. Excitement lifted her spirits. These houses were getting bigger and better. Maggie never dreamed she might be in a huge house.

Ben and Maude were pulling hard uphill to where the brick street ended. Her mouth dropped open. The biggest house she had ever seen graced the sky. It was taller than most of the trees that surrounded it. Majestic white pillars supported a wood balcony. This must be a mansion, she thought. She had never seen one, but this *had* to be a mansion. An airy whistle escaped without Maggie even knowing it. "Do you live in that?" she asked in awe.

Opal and Ruby giggled.

"Nope, but we've been in it. Mama works there," Opal explained.

"What does she do?" Maggie asked.

"Mostly cooks."

"Yep. Mama's a good cooker." Ruby rubbed her tummy.

"Ruby's always hungry. Must be growing, Mama says." Opal shook her head. "Sometimes Mama sews for them, too."

"Who are they?" Maggie asked.

"The Gatlins. They own just about everything in town. Mama says by the time this depression is over, they will be the only ones who own anything at all in Dodge City."

"Why?" wondered Maggie. She had heard a little about the depression, but her daddy didn't talk much about those things.

"Because Mr. Gatlin owns both the grocery stores in Dodge City, and he gives credit," Opal began.

"What's credit?"

"I had to ask Mama that, too. She says *credit* is when you don't have money. You have to sign your name on some sort of paper that says you promise to pay later for what you bought," Opal explained.

"You can really do that?" Maggie was in awe.

"Yep."

"Wow!"

"But, Mama says if you can't pay for your bill Mr. Gatlin will take your property." Opal spread her hands wide.

"Then why don't people just pay what they owe?" asked Maggie.

"Mama says if they had the money to pay, they would pay in the first place and not use credit. But they don't have the money and their families are hungry."

"That's exactly right, Opal. Hunger is hard to handle, and hungry children sometimes persuade mamas and daddies to make poor decisions. Using credit from Mr. Gatlin is a poor decision," Sue interrupted. "Most of the folks are banking on a crop. Thomas Gatlin is banking on a crop *failure*. So far he's winning."

Maggie knew that. There had been three long springs and summers in a row with no rain on their farm. No rain meant no crop and no harvest. No harvest meant no money for dresses or anything else. That was one of the reasons Daddy had packed up Maggie to come and marry Sue and live in the city. He said he needed a job to save the farm, and he hoped he could find one here. It would sure have to be a good paying job to make a living, Maggie thought. That is if he was to buy food for this new family and save the farm, too.

"We've been praying for rain," Opal continued, "but so far Mama says it's just like those empty clouds in the Bible."

"What clouds?" Maggie asked.

"You know, those big, old, black clouds that peek over the horizon, and everyone gets their hopes all built up. Then you watch them blow in, and when they finally get here, they are all full of dirt and wind without a drop of rain."

"It says that in the Bible?" Maggie questioned.

"Yep, it does." Opal took a deep breath and began to recite. " 'Whoso boasteth himself of a false gift is like clouds and wind without rain.' That is found in Proverbs chapter twenty-five and verse number fourteen."

Maggie looked skeptical. This girl must be older than the eight years she had guessed she was.

Opal continued, "Mama says Mr. Gatlin is like those clouds, too. He's promising something good, and there is no good in his promise."

"Just how old are you?" Maggie blurted.

"I'm nine going on twelve, Mama says."

"What does that mean?"

Opal shrugged her shoulders and changed the subject. "Oh, good, we're taking the shortcut. Mr. Gatlin lets us use it. I think he's sweet on Mama."

"He's sweet on your mama?"

"His first wife died and she was a friend to Mama. Mama says Mr. Gatlin wasn't very nice to his first wife and she sure wouldn't want to be his next wife," Opal sighed.

"Opal," Sue warned.

Maggie had more questions for Opal, but she didn't say anything else.

The wagon went through the gates of the Gatlin estate, then took a "Y" in the drive that swerved to the side of the mansion and around to the back. Maggie studied the house. Lace curtains hung at every single window. Behind the house there was a stable and a garage. A blue Hudson sat in the drive just outside the garage. "Have you ridden in that automobile?" Maggie's eyes were wide.

Opal nodded.

"Only once," Ruby whispered.

"Wow! Oh, wow!" whistled Maggie. This living in town might not be so bad after all.

They passed the stable and headed beyond. Maggie thought they were driving straight for the pasture. Daddy pulled up the team, handed the reins to Sue and dropped to the ground. Deftly he unlatched the gate and swung it wide. Sue guided the wagon through. Daddy closed the gate, jumped back on the wagon, and started the team across the pasture. A few hardy cottonwoods dotted the landscape and followed a dry creek bed. Against the far fence Maggie could see what looked to be a three-sided shed. The only other thing standing in this stretched-out pasture was a faded railroad boxcar.

"You live in the country?" Maggie asked.

"Yep, but Mama says it'll most likely be town one of these days."

"How much farther to where you live?"

Opal blinked. "This is it, right here." She pointed to the old boxcar.

"That?! That boxcar?" Maggie studied Opal's face. She didn't blink or move a muscle, so she must be telling the truth. "You live in that boxcar?"

Opal and Ruby nodded.

"This is the backside. The front side looks better because there's a porch along it. Mama says a coat of paint would help a whole bunch, but that's a someday thing," Opal explained.

Maggie watched as the wagon made its way around the side and to the front of the old boxcar. Opal was right. There was a porch strung across the front and it did make the boxcar a bit more inviting. But it was in dire need of paint and it sagged in the middle. The porch offered the luxury of being screened all the way around. It had its own door and another one that led inside from the porch. Windows had been cut in both the front and back of the boxcar home.

Sam slowed the wagon to a halt.

Sue smiled weakly. "I told you it wasn't much, Sam. It's small, but it's a warm place out of the cold," her voice dwindled.

"We aren't used to much, Sue. It will be fine. It'll be just fine. Cozy." Sam patted his new wife's hand.

Sue gave them a big smile. She took a deep breath and said, "Welcome home, Sam, Maggie. Welcome to your new home."

CHAPTER 3 — *Company*

Opal and Ruby dove out of the wagon. They were excited to be home and ready to show off all their work. "Come on, Maggie. Come see our house."

"House?" Maggie whispered. She never imagined anyone living in a boxcar. She hesitated, still staring at it. Slowly she slipped over the side of the wagon and dropped to the ground.

"Go on, Maggie," Sue urged from beside her. "The girls have been working really hard to get the house ready for you."

Maggie looked down and kicked at the dirt. If she went into this house, she had a sinking feeling it would become hers. *Maggie, the boxcar girl.* Her stomach rolled.

"Maggie, honey, go on inside. I'll be following as soon as I take care of Ben, Maude and Lulubelle." With a gentle shove, her daddy pushed her toward the screen door Opal was holding open.

Maggie trudged up the steps. The wood floor creaked with each movement. She closed her eyes, and with a deep breath, crossed the threshold of her new home. Once inside, she saw that the living room was tiny. A stove stood almost smack dab in the middle of the living area. A small table with crude benches took up most of the remaining space. The only other furniture was a little end table and a rocking chair.

"Come see our room!" exploded Opal. She pulled back an old quilt that had been nailed over the door on the east side of the living area. Inside the room, a bed was shoved up against the wall. It wasn't very big, Maggie noticed. If the three of them were to sleep together, it would be a tight fit. Her eyes dropped to the floor. Two pieces of firewood held up one side of the bed. It looked like the bed would fold right in the middle if you took out the wood. Opal followed her gaze. "The bed is kind of old, but it's new to us. Mama did some trading for it because she figured we needed a bigger bed than the old one. We fixed it best as we could."

Ruby threw in a suggestion. "Maybe our new daddy could fix it better."

Maggie glared at the floor, but she didn't say anything.

Opal did. "I'll bet he can fix things good, can't he, Maggie?"

"Yep," Maggie said. "He can do just about anything in this whole world. That wouldn't be hard for him at all."

Opal smiled. "See, Ruby, Mama told us having a daddy would come in handy."

Ruby giggled. Maggie didn't.

Opal stepped over to a small chest of drawers. "Mama had us clean out the top drawer for you. She said since you were older you would be taller, and we should give you the top drawer so you wouldn't have to be bending over all the time."

Maggie shrugged. "I could just keep my stuff in my carpet-bag. You could keep all your drawers then." She was afraid to unpack. Maybe Daddy would decide he had made a mistake, and if he did, she wanted to be ready to go.

"Well, suit yourself," Opal spread out her hands. "That's about it for our room." She studied the empty walls. "Oh, there are some nails if you want to hang some stuff."

Maggie nodded.

"Want to see our mama's room?"

Maggie bit her lower lip. For some dumb reason tears were building. This was just a place. Why was she having trouble with tears? Like a zombie she nodded her head and followed Opal through the quilt door, across the living room, and to an opening on the west side of the boxcar.

There was a door on this room, but it was an old screen door with cardboard nailed to it. Maggie was surprised this room was no bigger than the other bedroom. The bed was about the same size, but at least it had all four legs. Their mama had a beautiful old dressing table with a big mirror. The mirror was smoky, but it still held a good reflection. A square traveling trunk holding a lamp and a Bible stood on end at the side of the bed. It served as a night table.

"Do you think you should?" Sue's clear voice startled Maggie. The girls flooded the living room in time to watch Mr. Daniels pick up Sue and carry her through the porch door and then into the house. The three girls froze. In the silence that followed, Sam quickly set Sue down and slid the hat off his head. Sue straightened the front of her dress. "Uh, I'll get us something to eat."

"I'll get some water." Sam turned and walked out the door. As the screen door slammed behind him, a black sedan pulled into the drive. Sam called over his shoulder, "Sue, you've got company."

All three girls crowded through the door onto the porch and watched as the rice lady from church stepped out of her car. Her husband had eased out of the sedan and was following her up to the porch when he spied Mr. Daniels. The man stopped and headed toward Maggie's daddy. The woman didn't even knock. She just opened the door and hollered, "Sue, you home?"

Maggie thought that was a dumb question. She had just passed Daddy in the front yard by the pump and all three girls were within sight on the porch. Without waiting for Sue to answer, she stepped inside.

"Come on in, Mrs. Crenshaw," Sue invited. "I was just getting ready to start cooking. Do you and Jack want to have dinner with us?"

"Oh, goodness, no. We brought you a picnic lunch. There's enough for all of you, but if you and that new husband of yours want to take it and run, Jack and I would be glad to watch the kids for you." Mrs. Crenshaw set the picnic basket on the floor and dropped into the rocker.

"Mrs. Crenshaw, that's very sweet of you," Sue hugged her.

"I want to tell you that you gave me the shock of my life. Why, I was never so surprised. Just where did you meet this man, and how in the world have you kept him hidden from everyone, especially me? Why, I thought we were the best of friends. Why didn't you tell me about him?"

Maggie began to wonder if this Mrs. Crenshaw ever stopped to breathe.

Before Sue could assure Mrs. Crenshaw they *were* friends, Mrs. Crenshaw continued. "I will have to say, he is one handsome man. And would you ever believe it? He looks like he could be the father of your girls with all that dark hair of his. But that little girl . . . she doesn't look a thing like him. I wonder where she got her looks? And, Sue," Mrs. Crenshaw shook her head, "that dress the poor girl had on . . . why, it must have been three or four sizes too big, besides being as old as the hills. You sure have your work cut out for you!"

The tears Maggie had been fighting won the battle. She threw the screen door open, scrambled off the porch, and ran. She didn't know where to run, but she had to get away. If she thought she could get back to the farm, that's exactly where she would go. Deep in the pasture she found a huge cottonwood tree. She grabbed a low hanging limb and swung up into the branches. She continued to climb until she felt hidden from the world. Her storm of tears was the gully washer the farmers had been praying for to bless their thirsty land.

For Maggie, it was simply her heart ripped open, and she didn't know if she would ever be well again. She cried until there were no more tears. Her stomach wrenched and her body continued to tremble. She ached for her mama. Why did death happen? Daddy said God decided those things. He said God decided it was Mama's time to go. Well, Maggie didn't think very much of God. Daddy told her Mama wouldn't want to come back because she is in heaven, and heaven is a wonderful place. Maggie didn't think that could be possible. Why would Mama leave her? It didn't sound like Mama to Maggie. Sure, heaven was supposed to be a wonderful place, but not until you're ready to go.

Maggie watched the cottonwood leaves dance in the light wind. The leaves were shiny, and as they did their wind dance they glittered and made their own music. Maggie was so tired. The last few days had been hard. As her trembling body eased, a blanket of sleep slipped over her.

"Maggie! Maggie!"

As though using an ax to chop her way through a thick forest, Maggie fought to wake from the deep sleep.

"Maggie! Maggie!" She slowly opened her eyes and lifted her head from the rough branch where she was clinging.

"Maggie!"

"Daddy?"

Beneath the big cottonwood, Daddy had dropped his head. His strong hands clenched and unclenched. "Maggie, where are you, honey?"

"Daddy," Maggie called.

Slowly, Mr. Daniels raised his head to gaze into the tree. "Maggie?" He searched the depths.

"I'm here, Daddy," Maggie spoke quietly.

Daddy shook his head as his eyes settled on his little girl. "I should have known you'd find a tree to climb. Mama always said you were a monkey. She said you climbed before you walked."

"She did?"

Daddy nodded. "Can you get down?"

"Yes, Daddy." But Maggie didn't move.

"Are you *ready* to come down, Maggie?" Daddy asked.

"I guess so." Slowly Maggie made her way from branch to branch. She had climbed higher than she realized. Her body was stiff from holding onto the tree while she slept and it made her descent slow. When she finally dropped to the ground, Daddy's arms surrounded her. There were no more tears to cry, and in his arms was exactly where she wanted to be.

Daddy held her and let time stretch to grab at another day. Evening shadows played in the distance and finally gave way to darkness. He broke the silence. "Maggie, are you ready to go home?"

"I'm scared."

"I know, honey. It's okay to be scared. Sometimes your daddy is scared, too. It's what you do with the scared that makes the difference. You can let it ruin you or you can stand up brave-like and face it. That's what I want you to do right now. I want you to take a deep breath and walk with your head high. It might be hard, Maggie, but you can do it. I know you can because you have the same stubborn determination your mama had." He put his finger under her chin and raised it to look squarely into her eyes. "Now, chin up. Let's go home."

Together they walked through the dark pasture to their new boxcar home. A warm glow from the lamp invited them inside. Sue was waiting. Mrs. Crenshaw was gone.

"Are you all right, Maggie?" asked Sue.

Maggie nodded.

"Are you hungry?" Sue's eyes searched hers.

Maggie shook her head. She just wanted to sleep. When she slept, everything seemed to go away.

"Are you sure, Maggie?" Daddy questioned.

Maggie nodded her head. "Yes." She was so tired, she could barely speak.

"I think you better at least drink a cup of warm milk." Daddy left no room for argument.

"Okay."

Sue led Maggie to the rocker and turned to pour her a glass of milk. As she handed it to Maggie, Sue questioned Sam with her eyes. He shook his head with a *wait until later* look.

Maggie gulped the milk down. She didn't want any more questions, so she stood up. "Good night," she whispered as she went toward her room. As she raised the quilt door, her daddy strode over and kissed her on the forehead. "I love you, Maggie," he whispered.

"I love you, too, Daddy." She eased around the quilt.

From the bed, Opal spoke. Maggie jumped. Opal giggled. "We put your carpetbag under the window."

"Thanks." Maggie walked over to the window and gazed out into the moonlight.

"If you don't want to sleep on the edge, I'll trade places with you. Ruby's already asleep, but she likes being by the wall so she won't fall out of bed." Opal was a talker.

"The edge is fine." Maggie unpinned the neck of Mama's dress and slipped it over her head. Gently she folded it and laid it on top of her carpetbag, then dug for her nightgown. With one last, long look at the moon, she sighed. Could Mama see her from up there? She turned from the window and quickly slid into bed. She stayed on her edge, as far away from Opal as she could get.

CHAPTER 4

Snow Feathers

Sunlight soaked through the window. Maggie rolled over and stretched. When her foot hit a warm body, her heart stopped. Who was in bed with her? Terrified, she tumbled over the edge. Tangled covers bound her legs and she crashed to the floor. Wildly she kicked to set herself free. Her foot, in the wad of covers, smashed against the chunk of firewood that held up the bed. A mass of sheets, blankets, pillows, and little girls piled on top of her. Dazed, Maggie dug through to the top. Giggles ignited laughter.

Only Ruby didn't understand. "Why did you do that?" she demanded. To emphasize her feelings, she slammed her pillow on top of Opal's head.

"Hey!" Opal shouted, "I didn't do it." She grabbed the pillow out of Ruby's hands and walloped her with it. Then, to show her innocence, she pointed to Maggie. "She did it!" Opal swung the pillow and Maggie fell back to the heap in the floor, but she didn't stay there. She pulled another pillow from the pile and entered the battle. Feathers took flight that hadn't flown since they'd known a bird. The girls danced from floor to bed and back again—the laughter reverberating against the walls. The fight raged.

Sue stood at the door. "Just what are you girls doing?"

Sam looked in and then backed out of the room. This looked like a matter for Sue to handle. Frankly, he didn't know about such things as girls' squabbles—and he didn't want to learn.

Silence and feathers settled over the girls.

Sue studied each of them. "Opal?"

Opal swallowed, her eyes wide. "I didn't start it," she whispered.

"Ruby?" Sue looked deep into the little girl's eyes.

Quickly she shook her head. "All I know is that I woke up on the floor—and I don't like the floor."

"You did not! You were on top of me and I am not the floor!" Opal crossed her arms and tried to tap her foot while still standing on top of the bed. She lost her balance and tumbled into Ruby. Together they fell—shoving Maggie. Maggie toppled backwards. The pillow she held tightly swung over her head, smacked Sue and exploded. Once more the room was a snowstorm of feathers. Maggie gasped and tried to stumble to her feet.

From the floor, Sue sputtered feathers. Silence. Pillow stuffing slowly continued to fall in the room. No one dared breathe as all eyes rested on Sue. Maggie shook. She hadn't meant to hit Sue. She hadn't meant to knock the firewood out from under the bed. It was all an accident, but would anyone ever believe that?

"Sam!" Sue called.

Maggie froze. Just what would Daddy do when he found

out Maggie had kerwalloped Sue?

"Yes?" Sam ducked his head under the quilt.

Sue eyed the girls. "Sam, are you any good at fixing roofs?"

"I suppose." He studied her.

"Good. As you can see, it must have snowed last night, and there must be one huge hole in the roof. It needs to be fixed before winter sets in," Sue's eyes twinkled.

Daddy nodded, "I'll be doin' that right away."

Sue was the first one to laugh. It didn't take long for everyone to join her. Maggie didn't understand, but she was glad her heart could start beating again.

Sue stood and brushed the feathers to the floor. "Girls, after breakfast I want these pillows restuffed and sewn back together. I want this room cleaned," she paused, "and no more pillow fights. Too many good birds lost their lives to give you the luxury of sleeping on nice soft pillows. Is that understood?"

Opal was the first to answer, "Yes, ma'am."

Ruby followed, "Yes, ma'am."

Sue looked at Maggie. Quickly she nodded in agreement and repeated, "Yes, ma'am." If she had wondered what to call Sue, this settled it for her. She could just call her *ma'am*. She had known all along there was no way Daddy would settle for Maggie calling her new mama *Sue*. So far she had been lucky and hadn't needed to speak to her at all, but she had known it wouldn't last.

"You girls get dressed now and come on to breakfast." Sue turned and left the girls alone.

"Whew! I'm sure glad you're here, Maggie. Mama is never that easy on us." Opal sank down on the floor with relief.

"Me, too! Usually I get my buns spanked." Ruby rubbed

hers to show Maggie just where the spankings were applied.

"Yep, Mama says it's the seat of knowledge." Opal's lips formed a grim line.

"You ever get spankings?" Ruby asked.

Maggie shrugged her shoulders. "Doesn't everyone?"

"Mama says if you are loved, you will get spankings," Ruby told her.

"Then consider me loved," Opal threw her hands in the air. "I can't figure how that works, though," she added.

"Well, it's because God's Word says it. You know that, Opal. Mama keeps telling you," Ruby reminded her.

"I know, Ruby. I just don't understand it." Opal faced her little sister.

"Mama . . . " Ruby began but her sister shushed her.

Opal ran her finger across her throat. "I don't want to hear any more about it, Ruby. Now get dressed."

Ruby pulled off her nightgown. "I'll bet we hear more about it."

Opal muttered under her breath something about sisters.

Maggie shoved her mama's dress to the floor and dug for her clothes in her carpetbag. Quickly she slid out of her night-clothes and into her everyday wear. She snapped the loop over the button and turned. Both girls were staring at her.

"You wear overalls?" Ruby asked.

Maggie felt a rush of red spread over her cheeks.

"Your daddy lets you wear overalls?" Ruby shook her head in disbelief.

"Ruby! Hush your big, fat mouth! You know she hasn't had a mama to teach her those things, and Mama told us daddies don't know how to teach little girls stuff like that," Opal scolded

Ruby.

Maggie just stood. The only dress she had was the rosebud dress of Mama's that lay wadded on the floor now, and she guessed she knew what people thought of *that*. The overalls had come from the neighbors down the road. They had boys and Maggie had needed clothes. Overalls had been her dress now for three years. Still Maggie stood.

Ruby walked over to Maggie and looked up at her. "I'm sorry, Maggie. I guess it just shocked the liver out of me." She was so matter of fact and so honest that Maggie smiled. Ruby slid her hand into Maggie's. "Come on. Let's go eat, because I am a starving girl."

Sue raised her eyebrows a bit as she noticed Maggie's attire, but she didn't say a word. She placed a plate of hotcakes in the middle of table. "Girls, you slide together on the back bench. I'll bet you can squeeze together just fine. Ruby gets the middle." She left no room for argument.

Sam waited for Sue to sit down, then he eased in beside her. "It sure looks and smells good, Sue."

"Thanks, Sam. You want to say grace?" she asked.

"Sure." Sam bowed his head, "Father, we thank you for this wonderful day and this wonderful food. We would ask you to walk with us and keep us in your hands today." Sam paused, "And Father, I want to thank you for my new family."

Maggie's head popped up. Prayer was a private thing for Daddy. Hearing him was a rare thing and her heart wasn't ready for him to be so thankful about this new family. She ate in silence.

"Girls," Sue began, "just what did happen this morning?" Her eyes were on Maggie.

Maggie guessed Ruby was right and they hadn't heard the last of it yet. She swallowed the bite of pancakes and took a swig of milk. She looked to her daddy who nodded for her to explain.

"Well, I didn't mean for all of that to happen. When I woke up, I forgot where I was and I felt someone in bed beside me. I got scared and tried to jump up. I got all tangled and then I fell out of bed and knocked the log out from under the end. Then Opal and Ruby were dumped on top of me. I really don't know what happened from there." Maggie's eyes were huge.

"Girls?" Sue looked at them. Opal and Ruby shrugged. "Well," Sue hesitated, "that was about the funniest sight I have ever seen. Pass the hotcakes." Sue stabbed another one and handed it to her husband.

Maggie couldn't figure Sue out. Mostly she was expecting to get into trouble. Maybe if she just kept quiet, things would be okay.

"Maggie?" Sue asked.

Here it comes, she thought. "Yes, ma'am?" The word felt funny on her heart.

"I want you to bring me all of your dresses after breakfast." Sue was studying her.

"She ain't got but one," Ruby chimed in.

"Keep your mouth shut, Ruby." Opal jabbed her in the ribs and whispered between clenched teeth, but everyone heard it.

"Listen to your sister, Ruby," Sue told her.

Maggie almost choked.

"Then Maggie, bring me your dress after breakfast. We'll have a fitting session before I go to work this morning, and we'll see if we can't get that pretty dress to fit this pretty young lady. Will that be a fine thing with you, Maggie?"

Maggie stared. Then she turned a questioning gaze to her daddy.

"I think it sounds like a mighty fine idea, Sue. I wish we could have done it before yesterday. It'll be right pretty on a right pretty young lady." Daddy winked at Maggie.

Maggie felt like crying. Sue didn't feel the same way that Mrs. Crenshaw woman felt. She fumbled with her fork. Was everything going to be as good as Daddy had promised?

"Maggie," Sue interrupted her thoughts. "If you're finished, go in and put your dress on and we'll get started. I'm a bit late. Your daddy's going to drop me at the Gatlin place on his way to look for a job."

Maggie slipped from the table and went to her new bedroom. Under the window—in a pile—was Mama's dress. Maggie picked it up and shook it. She pulled it over her head. This time she didn't use the safety pin and she kicked the old brown belt to the side. Smoothing down the dress, she felt the compact in her pocket. She snatched it out and started to drop it on top of her bag. No, she'd better tuck it in real good so nothing would happen to it.

Deep down under all of her clothes, she placed it with the rest of her treasures and patted it for safe keeping. Her finger caught on a thin round band of metal. She didn't have to pull it out to know it was her mama's wedding ring—Daddy's promise to love her mama the rest of his life. Now she guessed it didn't mean anything to Daddy. But it did to her. She would keep it with her treasures forever. She piled her clothes on top of Mama's things, then latched the carpetbag. With these things she could keep Mama close to her forever.

CHAPTER 5

Ask the Stars

"**D**o you always stay here when your mama goes to work?" Maggie wanted to know.

"We're just across the pasture." Opal wiped the last dish and put it away.

"But you're here all by yourself and you're just kids," Maggie squinted at them.

"I'm more than half grown. Mama got married when she was seventeen. That's only eight years away for me. If you look at it that way, I'm over half there. And look at all the things I can do. I can keep the fire going, I can cook a bunch of things, and I can sew." Opal was proud of her accomplishments.

"You can sew?" Maggie asked.

"Yep. I can show you, too. Besides, we got to fix our pillows," Opal reminded her.

"Opal?" Maggie waited until she turned to face her. "What happened to your daddy?"

Opal's memories dragged her from the present to the past. Remembering, her eyes had a faraway look and she seemed

much older than her nine years.

Snapping back to the present, Opal said, "Tell you what, let's get our pillows and Mama's sewing basket, and we'll talk." She walked to the disaster site and called, "Ruby, you got all those feathers gathered yet?"

"Most of them." Ruby chased a floating feather through the air.

"Good. We got to get them sewed before Mama comes home."

They gathered all their supplies and went out to the porch to work. Learning to sew wasn't hard for Maggie. She was quick with her hands. Maggie wanted to know about the girls' daddy, but she wasn't going to ask again. She would just wait until Opal felt comfortable enough to talk. It was something that hurt and she didn't mean to hurt Opal.

"Now, Ruby, remember you can't use the scissors when Mama's gone, so when you need something cut, you have to have either Maggie or me do it for you." Opal threaded a needle and handed it to Ruby. Ruby nodded.

Opal picked up her own sewing and continued. "Daddy was killed in an automobile explosion. He was putting gasoline in a customer's car and talking at the same time. Anyway, it ran over and splashed on the customer's shoes. The customer jumped back and dropped his cigarette right in the puddle of gasoline. Daddy was standing in it when it burst into flames. They said the gas hose was dragging in the puddle and the nozzle was still in the tank. The fire just followed the hose and the whole car exploded." She paused. "So did our daddy." Maggie didn't know what to say. She was sorry she had even asked, but it was too late now.

Opal continued, "Daddy died right away. I guess that makes me feel better, and it seems to help that it was a long time ago."

"How long?" Maggie felt she could ask that question.

"Ruby was a baby. She wasn't even a year old. That means I wasn't but three, so I don't remember too much about him. Mama tells us things, though, because she says that keeps him alive in our hearts and she doesn't want us to forget him. It's the only way we will know him." Opal smiled into the distance.

"I like your daddy," said Ruby.

Maggie forgot Ruby was even there. *Daddy* was *her* daddy, but that horrible gut feeling she had felt about sharing him didn't well up inside of her this time.

"I like him, too, Ruby," Maggie smiled slightly.

"I think he might be a little like our daddy was or Mama wouldn't have married him. Mr. Gatlin wanted to marry Mama but Mama wouldn't," Opal confided.

"He's the one with the mansion, isn't he?" asked Maggie.

"Yep. That's the guilty one," nodded Opal.

Maggie's jaw dropped in disbelief. "Why didn't she marry him? You could be living in that big house and I'll bet you could have had anything you wanted!"

It was Ruby that spoke, "Not you."

Maggie stared at Ruby. "Not me?" Maggie whispered.

Ruby reached over and laid her hand on Maggie's. "I like having you here."

"Yep. We never got by with a pillow fight before," Opal giggled.

When the laughter settled, Maggie persisted. "Really, why didn't your mama marry Mr. Gatlin?"

Opal tipped her head to one side, "Mama says it wasn't God's will."

"How does she know what God's will is?" Maggie scrunched her eyebrows together.

"She reads her Bible and talks to God," Ruby told her.

"Yep. The Bible says you aren't supposed to be unequally yoked with unbelievers," Opal explained.

"Yolked? *Egged?*" Maggie had no idea what Opal meant.

Opal shook her head and laughed. "Other kind of yoke. You know, like when your daddy plows, and he hitches the horses together?"

"Hitched? Hitched is yoked? So that's why hitched means married. I never knew that." Maggie's face lit up with understanding.

"Exactly right. Honestly, I never thought about the hitched and being married before, but it makes sense—along with what the Bible says," Opal nodded in agreement.

"How?"

"Well, Mama says it like this," Opal began. "Did you ever see your daddy hitch up Lulubelle and Ben to pull that wagon?"

Maggie shook her head, "I don't think they would work very well together. They would always be fighting with each other because Lulubelle is an old cantankerous cow and Ben is a work horse."

"Yep. One's a cow and one's a horse, and they don't think alike. A person who knows the Lord and one who doesn't— well, they don't think alike either—because they are different creatures. God tells us they shouldn't be hitched up together. It won't work." Opal finished sewing her pillow, tied a knot, and bit the thread.

Maggie was quiet. There was a lot in what Opal had said that made sense, but there were a few things she still didn't understand. She was amazed Sue had chosen to marry Daddy when she could have married Thomas Gatlin. With Daddy they could be living in this tiny boxcar the rest of their lives. Mr. Gatlin could have given her anything she wanted. Well, she smiled, except for Maggie—*if Sue wanted Maggie.*

"How'd your mama die?" Ruby asked.

Opal dropped the lid to her mama's sewing box. "Hush it up, Ruby! Mama warned you not to ask questions about Maggie's mama."

"It's okay." Maybe it would help Maggie to talk about it. There hadn't been one single soul who had ever asked her in all the three years since her mother's death. Daddy never had even said anything unless Maggie had asked. The couple of times she *had* asked, he had looked so pained she had decided not to question him anymore. She tightly hugged the pillow she was mending and then began.

"The Martins' bull got in our back pasture and moseyed into the pond. He got stuck out in the middle and was bawling something dreadful. I ran and told Mama. Mama roped him and tried to pull him out, but it ended up spooking the bull instead. There was an awful lot of splashing and noise. Then that old bull let out a bellow and reared up. When he came down, he landed on Mama. She couldn't get up. She couldn't get out of the water. I yelled, but no one heard me. I ran and found Daddy, but it was too late. I think I should have gone in the water after her, but I was scared of the bull. I tried to ask Daddy if it was my fault, but he just shook his head and looked away—far away." Maggie was crying, but she didn't know it.

She rocked back and forth hugging the pillow.

Ruby scooted close to Maggie and put her arm around her.

Opal's eyes were full. "Maggie, it wasn't your fault. You need to believe that. Your daddy told you that, and your daddy wouldn't lie to you, would he?" Maggie shook her head. Still the tears rolled.

"It's okay to cry. Mama says it's good to cry because it kind of washes the soul and gets it refreshed. Besides, Jesus cried. If Jesus can cry, then Mama says we can most certainly enjoy a good cry and not feel bad about it."

Opal was full of things her mama had said and that made Maggie cry all the more. She would never be full of the things her mama had said. She was only eight when Mama had been rudely jerked from her life, and with it she had taken any wisdom she ever would have imparted to Maggie. The load of guilt Maggie carried had often been taken to the stars—because somewhere way out in the stars was heaven—and that's where Mama lived. Maggie had asked the stars many times if she had killed Mama, but the stars never answered; and Maggie always turned away still bearing her heavy load. Could no one ever help her?

"Maggie?" Opal reached into her thoughts. "Listen to me." Gently Opal put both her hands on Maggie's cheeks and looked directly into her eyes. "Maggie, if Lulubelle got in the pond and you went in to pull her out, and somehow she fell on you, would you want Ruby to come into the pond to try to get Lulubelle off of you?"

With disbelief Maggie groaned, "No."

"Why?" Opal persisted.

"Ruby's too little. She would be too little to get Lulubelle off of me, and she would end up getting killed, too."

"Maggie, do you think your mama wanted you to come into that pond after her?" Opal's eyes never left Maggie's face.

Slowly understanding sank clear to the bottom of Maggie's heart.

Opal wasn't finished yet. "Maggie, do you think your daddy wanted you to go into that water to help your mama?"

A light shone from Maggie's heart. "No," she whispered.

"Maggie, I just know if your mama could answer, she would tell you it wasn't your fault, and that she didn't want you to come into the pond to try to help her. Maggie, do you understand?" asked Opal.

"Oh, yes." Maggie buried her head in the pillow. The wave of relief that swept over her carried her into the deepest calm she had ever known. She knew. She knew what she had done was okay. Mama wouldn't blame her, but what about Daddy? She knew Daddy wouldn't have wanted her to go into the water, but should she have gone to tell him in the first place—instead of Mama? Maggie drew in her breath and whispered, "Once at Mama's grave I heard Daddy say he wished I had come to tell him about our bull being stuck in the pond." Maggie's heart pounded in her ears, drowning out the voices of Opal and Ruby trying to drag her back. She shoved the devastating memory—and Opal and Ruby—far away in her mind as she buried her head in her knees. Maggie couldn't think about this right now. She was too tired. She slowly closed her eyes and began to sink further from her world.

While Ruby stroked Maggie's hair with her fingers, Opal grabbed a light blanket and spread it over Maggie. She continued sinking—not into the water she wished she had gone into in order to save her mama—but into sleep, right there on the floor in the middle of the porch.

CHAPTER 6

The God in Your Heart

*T*he screen door slammed. Sue crossed the porch, opened the house door, and went inside. Maggie struggled to pull her eyes open as she heard voices and tried to listen, yet it felt so good to lie here and let time slide by. It seemed as if all the talking was coming from another world, as she slowly let her eyes drift shut again.

"Girls, you left a mess on the porch," Sue called.

"That ain't a *mess*, Mama. It's Maggie," Ruby told her.

"It *isn't*." Sue corrected.

Maggie's eyes popped open as a tingly feeling surged through her. Sisters gave her a warmth she had never had before. She stretched so she could peek though the screen door. Maggie smiled at Ruby's *"ain't/isn't"* mistake. She knew Ruby would catch on pretty soon.

"*Isn't*, Ruby. We don't use the word *ain't*. It is not proper." Maggie watched as Sue lifted Ruby's chin and looked into her eyes.

"Okay. It *isn't* a mess—it's Maggie," Ruby was careful to use the right word this time.

"Much better. Now, Ruby, why is Maggie in a pile on the porch?" asked Sue.

Ruby shrugged, "I guess it's because we were talking, and she got started crying, and she just went to sleep."

Sue put her hand to her head. "Girls. I told you to be very careful of the things you say to Maggie; and especially to be careful of the questions you ask. You could really hurt her."

"Well, she asked us first," Opal defended herself.

Sue crossed to the rocker and sat down. "Just what did she ask?"

Opal began, "Maggie asked me how our daddy died—so I told her."

Sue pressed her lips together. "Then let me guess, you asked her how her mama died. Right?"

Ruby gasped, "How'd you know that?"

"Because she's a mama and mamas know everything, Ruby," Opal rolled her eyes.

"Yes girls, they do—and don't you forget it," Sue chuckled. "Now, I wonder just how much damage was done."

Opal shrugged. "Mama, do you know how Maggie's mama died?"

"I know it was with a bull in their pond and that it was an awful accident. I really know very little, though," Sue answered.

"Did you know Maggie saw it happen?" asked Opal.

"Oh no," Sue groaned. "What a horrible thing for a little girl to see."

"She thinks it was her fault, Mama. She thinks she should have gone into the water to try to get her mama free from the bull," Opal added.

"Poor, poor Maggie. There would have been nothing she

could have done except get herself killed, too." Sue's voice caught on a sob. "Maggie needs us so much, girls."

Maggie felt her heart pounding. She couldn't believe Sue didn't blame her for what had happened and that Sue wanted to help her. Maggie snuggled deeper into the blanket, but the warmth she felt came from inside herself, not from the extra covering.

"Mama, Maggie thinks her daddy might feel it is all her fault." Opal's voice held quiet sorrow.

"Honey, why does Maggie feel that way?" Sue wanted to know.

"Because she heard him talking at the grave. He said he wished Maggie would have come and gotten him instead of going to get her mama," Opal explained.

Sue took a deep breath. "I see. Probably her daddy did wish she had come to get him, but he's just pulling straws out of the air. He must have thought he could have gotten the bull out without getting hurt. But that is just a thought. God's will has to be considered. He tells us there is a time to be born and a time to die."

"But, Mama, that time hurts." Opal creased her brow.

"Yes, honey, it does. When we love someone and lose them, that separation hurts. But God promises we will see them again if we both know the Lord. God also tells us that better is the day of one's death than the day of one's birth."

"I'm not sure I understand and I'll just bet Maggie wouldn't agree with it." Opal shook her head in doubt.

Out on the porch Maggie thought about what Sue was saying. Your death was supposed to be better than your birth? That sounded crazy. If God really did say that, he had never

watched someone he loved die. There was no way watching someone you love die could make you believe dying is better than being born.

"Well, Opal, Ruby," Sue began, "it does depend on if you know the Lord. You see, girls, Jesus is not just God somewhere up there in outer space. He is Jesus, your Savior, living in your heart. So you have heaven to look forward to when you die. All the cares of this world are gone and you will be in the presence of Jesus forever. Dying is like being born into heaven and that is much better than being born onto earth. That is why God says the day of one's death is better than the day of one's birth."

Maggie thought about what she had just heard. She could understand a little bit how heaven was a better place for Mama to be than here on earth, but she didn't understand what the difference was between God being in outer space and Jesus living in your heart. Just how was he supposed to *get* into your heart? And just what was he going to do if he *got* in there? Maggie shook her head. Maybe these things were only for adults to understand.

"Does that help you understand, girls?" Sue asked.

"Yep," Opal chimed in.

Opal understood? Maggie scrunched her brow.

"Good. Now let's talk a minute about Maggie and her daddy. I know he cannot possibly blame Maggie for her mama's death. He loves Maggie too much. What he said about Maggie coming to get him instead of her mama was a wish, not *blame*. Maggie's daddy is a good man and he loves the Lord. I know he was hurt badly by Maggie's mama's death but he would never blame Maggie. He just plain loves her too much. Really, that is why he married me."

"Maggie's daddy married *you* because he loved *her?*" Ruby

tipped her head to the side.

"What?" Opal questioned.

"How does that make sense?" Maggie whispered to herself, but she strained her ears to hear more.

Sue nodded. "Maggie's daddy wrote to me. He explained how he badly needed a mama for his little girl because she was growing into a lady. Maggie's aunt in New Jersey offered to take Maggie, but she didn't want her daddy there to interfere with Maggie's raising. Maggie's aunt wanted him to put Maggie on the train and let her go. New Jersey is a long way and her daddy just couldn't do it. He did pray about it, though."

Maggie gasped. She didn't know. Daddy had never breathed a word about it to her. How horrible that would have been.

"Mama, how did Maggie's daddy know you?"

"Actually, he's a second cousin to Thomas Gatlin—except he's on the side with no money. It seems Mr. Gatlin tried to buy Maggie's daddy's farm for a little bit of nothing and it made him mad. He told Mr. Gatlin he'd see the bank take it before he'd let him have it. Anyway, while they were talking Mr. Gatlin mentioned he intended to marry me, and he proceeded to tell Maggie's daddy all about me. So Maggie's daddy began writing to me. I'm not sure of the reason he wrote at first. It could have been just a way to get back at his cousin, but he did need a mama for Maggie. And I needed a daddy for the two of you." Sue patted each of her daughters on the head.

"But you didn't even hardly know him," Opal spoke quietly.

"You never, ever saw him before?" Ruby's eyes were huge.

"No, but I do know the Lord. Opal, Ruby, I wouldn't go into this marriage without praying about it. Maggie's daddy wouldn't either. I know the important things about him.

Number one, he knows the Lord. Number two, he loves Maggie. Number three, he has no respect for Thomas Gatlin!" Sue laughed. Ruby and Opal joined her.

Maggie wondered even more about this Thomas Gatlin.

"Are you sorry, Mama?" Opal asked.

"No. Sometimes it's scary, but if it is what God wants you to do, then you just walk in the grace God gives, and you can do it. He will give you the strength and courage to do what he asks." Sue hesitated a moment before she asked them, "Are *you* sorry?"

Opal was the first to answer, "No, I like having a daddy."

Ruby whispered, "I like having Maggie."

Maggie didn't know what was wrong with her. Again her heart was squeezing the tears from her eyes. She was feeling emotions she couldn't identify. She liked the escape she had found in sleep, but she didn't feel like running anymore. She needed some thinking time to figure out some of the things she had just heard.

Quietly she crawled from under the blanket, folded it, and laid it on top of the pillow. Still she sat—her mind running with questions. She never had the freedom to talk to her daddy like Opal and Ruby talked to their mama. Was it because he was a daddy? Would she have been able to talk to her own mama like that? Would she ever be able to talk to Sue like that? Maggie shivered. Sure, Sue said she knew she was in God's will, and she was pretty sure Daddy was in God's will, but what about Maggie? Just because they were in God's will, did it make her in it, too? And Sue had said God would help you be strong if you were doing what he wanted you to do. Maggie took a deep breath. She had made a decision. She was going to ask her daddy if he thought it was her fault Mama died.

Maggie squeezed her eyes tight and prayed. "Dear God, not the outer space God, but the one that comes to live in your heart God, please help me to ask my daddy about my mama. Please, please, please, God. Amen." She unscrunched her eyes and whistled. This God answered fast! Daddy was driving up the lane right now.

Opal Trouble

aggie jumped from the porch floor. She crossed to the screen door and stopped. Could she really ask Daddy if he thought it was her fault Mama had died? Maggie had always been able to talk with Daddy about the horses, and Lulubelle, and the weather, but this was a whole different thing. She drew in a deep breath and slowly let it out. Sue had said the God that lives in hearts could help you do anything, and she had just asked him to help her. She pushed through the door and down the steps. Daddy didn't stop at the boxcar home. Maggie paused. He headed the team straight for the lean-to shed without even turning to look at the house. That didn't seem like Daddy. He would have at least smiled and waved. Maybe this wasn't a good time to ask, but it was imbedded in her heart now and she couldn't let it go. She tromped down the dusty path behind the wagon.

At the lean-to, Daddy pulled the horses to a halt and jumped from the wagon. Maggie could hear him talking and she glanced around. No one was there, so she figured he must be talking to the horses. Daddy always told her it was good to talk to animals because it calms them down. Maggie eased closer.

"Lord, I don't have an understanding of a lot of things, but this beats them all. Right now I feel like I could explode. If he was close there's no telling just what I'd do to him." Daddy jammed his fists into the palm of his hand.

Maggie backed away. Daddy wasn't talking to the horses. He was talking to God and it didn't sound like a conversation she wanted to interrupt. Daddy was mad and that was a good time to leave him alone. As she started back to her new home she wondered who he was mad at and what had happened in town today. Maybe she should have stayed and listened a little longer. Maggie shook her head. No, she could learn things she didn't want to know, plus she could get in big trouble if she got caught. She kicked at the dirt as she trudged down the path. Her heart dropped. Maggie couldn't be with Daddy right now and she really didn't want to go to the house. She stopped and stood still for a long time—then slowly sank to the dust and just sat there. She wished she were home—not this home, *her* home.

"Maggie! Maggie!" Ruby stumbled through the door and down the steps. "Maggie! Your daddy's home." Ruby stopped in her tracks, "Hey, Maggie, are you all right?" She dropped down beside her new sister.

"Yeah, Ruby, I'm all right," Maggie lied. She didn't know if she would ever be all right again.

"Yeah? Then how come you're sitting in the dirt?" Ruby asked.

"You're sitting in the dirt, too."

"That's because you're sitting in the dirt," Ruby scrunched her brows together.

Maggie giggled. Ruby didn't. "Okay, Ruby. I'm thinking," Maggie told her.

"Right here in the dirt—in the middle of here?" Ruby spread her hands. Maggie laughed.

"You girls hatching eggs?" Daddy had slipped up behind the girls and both of them jumped.

Ruby giggled. "Maggie's thinking and I'm watching her do it."

Daddy raised his brows in question. "Never could understand women." He tousled Maggie's hair and winked at Ruby. "Anything to eat in the house?" he asked.

"It's fixing." Ruby scrambled up and brushed the dust from her dress.

"Well, let's go check it out." Daddy turned toward the house, "You two coming or do I get your share?"

"Not my share you don't." Ruby put her hands on her hips. "My mama's fixing biscuits and gravy and that's some of the best stuff in this here whole world."

"Well then, you'd best be headed that way because as soon as I wash up, I'm for eating." Daddy winked over Ruby's head at Maggie. Ruby took off for the house.

Maggie studied Daddy. He didn't look mad now. Maybe she could ask him her question. She watched him walk over to the pump, heft up the pump handle, and smash it down. She thought he used a lot more strength than he needed. She crept up beside him. With each downward stroke of the pump handle, Daddy whispered between his teeth. "Thomas Gatlin! The Lord help your soul the day you die!" Water came gushing out of the spout. Daddy filled the bucket and dunked his head into it. Maggie backed away. Thomas Gatlin? He had made Daddy mad? Daddy pulled his head from the bucket and shook it like a wet dog. Maggie giggled as the spray showered over her.

"Maggie?" Daddy wiped his face with his hands and smiled. "I didn't know you were there, pumpkin."

"Daddy . . . ?" Maggie began.

"Supper. Come get it while it's hot," Opal called.

"Well, Maggie, shall we go and get it while it's hot?" Daddy stretched his hand out to her. Maggie nodded and swallowed the question she had been ready to blurt out.

Ruby was right. Sue was a good cook. Even though there was very little sausage in the gravy it tasted better than any Maggie had ever made. The biscuits were warm and flaky and Maggie thought she could eat a dozen of them.

Opal and Ruby jabbered at the table, but for the most part Maggie was quiet. So were Sue and Daddy. Oh, they smiled and asked questions about little things, but they weren't really talking. It seemed to Maggie there was something both of them wanted to say, but neither one of them knew how to say it. Finally, at the end of supper, Daddy leaned back from the table and eyed all of the girls. "Ladies, Sue and I haven't had much time together today and I was wondering if you would mind going outside to play. Of course that would mean you would have to miss out on the dishes, and I know you would hate that."

"No, we wouldn't!" Ruby bubbled.

"Then that would be okay with you ladies?" Daddy raised his brows.

"You bet!" Ruby jumped from the bench and would have sent it sliding across the floor if Opal and Maggie hadn't weighted it down.

"Whoa, Ruby!" Opal complained.

"Girls, maybe you'd rather stay and clean up, and we can go for a walk?" Sue asked.

"No!" Again Ruby was the one to answer.

Daddy laughed, "Then if you ladies will excuse us?"

The three girls tumbled out the door. Opal was the first one to talk. "You know what this means, don't you?"

"We get out of the dishes tonight," giggled Ruby.

Opal rolled her eyes, "Besides that, Ruby." Ruby shrugged her shoulders.

"What?" Maggie whispered.

"I'll tell you what it means," Opal began. "It means they have some real important stuff they want to talk about, but they don't want us to know what it is."

"So?" Ruby crossed her arms.

Maggie's eyes grew wide as she realized Opal was right. Her heart began to beat a bit faster and her stomach started to churn. If it was something Sue and Daddy didn't want them to know, it must be something bad. Or maybe Daddy had decided this marriage wasn't a good idea after all and he wanted to tell Sue alone. Maggie felt sorry for Sue.

Opal had her arms crossed, "You know what we could do?" Maggie shook her head. Opal looked into the distance and licked her lips, "We could go listen at the back window."

Ruby stomped her foot. "Opal, that would be wrong and you know it!"

"Can you get close enough to the window to hear?" Maggie kicked at the ground. She didn't feel right about listening. Eavesdropping was what it was really called. Although if Opal thought it was all right, maybe it wouldn't be so bad.

Opal nodded, "There's an old water trough we could tip over and slide under the window. If we were real quiet, I think it would work. At least we could try," she said, her eyes pleading with them to go along.

"Okay." Maggie slid her clammy hands down the sides of her overalls. In her heart she knew it was wrong to listen, but she wanted badly to know what was so secret they needed to talk alone.

"You guys are going to do it?" Ruby opened her mouth wide.

"Ruby," Opal turned to explain to her, "it's for our own good. Besides, they are probably going to try to find a way to tell us anyway. This will help them because we will already know. They won't have to try so hard to explain it to us. Right, Maggie?"

Maggie pulled her gaze from the ground. "Right," she agreed.

"Okay." Opal fixed her eyes on Ruby, "You've got to promise to never breathe a word of this as long as you live. If you do I guarantee you won't live long! Now promise!"

"Okay, but I ain't going to listen," Ruby glared at Opal.

"Good. Now shake," Opal demanded. Ruby squinted, spit in her hand, and reached out toward her sister. Opal grabbed Ruby's hand and shook it. Then she dropped it and swiped her hand alongside her dress. "Let's get to work."

With a lot of tugging the girls managed to tip and slide the old water trough into place beneath the window. Opal and Maggie crawled on top of the trough while Ruby slipped to the shade of a nearby cottonwood and began playing with a June bug. "What they are doing is wrong, Mr. June Bug, and I don't like it. That Opal gets me into lots of trouble and I'll just bet you she's fixing to get me into trouble again. And poor, poor Maggie. She's going to get a good old dose of Opal Trouble!"

The June bug crawled from one finger to another while Ruby continued to confess.

Opal and Maggie stretched on their toes to peek inside. Daddy had a dish towel thrown over his shoulder and a dry plate in his hand. Sue looked like she could burst into tears at any moment. "Sam, he fired me."

Sam set the plate on the table. "Why?"

Sue shook her head. "Oh, he said some horrible, awful things . . ."

"What things?" Sam interrupted.

"Oh, Sam, I couldn't," Sue looked at the floor.

"Sue," Sam took her by the shoulders. Then he gently put his fingers under her chin and lifted it so their eyes would meet. "Sue, we are husband and wife. No secrets. That was something both of us agreed on, remember?"

Sue nodded, "Thomas Gatlin fired me because he said our marriage was on questionable grounds."

"Questionable grounds? Just how does he figure that?"

"He said there is a three-day waiting period here, and that you're of no account, and there wasn't a ring to prove anything, and I can't even remember everything else he said," she stuttered to a halt.

"But the preacher wouldn't have married us if it wasn't legal. And as for my being of no account, that is just a matter of opinion, and his opinion isn't worth a hill of beans to me. Now, the ring thing—Sue, he was just trying to make you feel bad. Lots of people are married and have no rings to prove it." He studied her eyes. "I am sorry there is no ring. In time we'll get you one. I even tried to find Margaret's ring. I hoped you wouldn't mind wearing it until we could afford a special one for you, but it was nowhere to be found. I didn't think they buried it with her but maybe they did. I don't remember everything that went on then."

Outside on the porch, Maggie closed her eyes. Her stomach churned. Daddy had been going to give Mama's wedding ring to Sue? She felt like her mama's grave had been ripped open. How could Daddy want to do that?

"Sam, the ring doesn't matter," Sue's voice shook. "It's the job. He isn't even going to let me finish the week. Not only that, he told me there wouldn't be a single soul in Dodge City who would take me on with my questionable character."

Sam pulled Sue into his arms. "Maybe God wants you to stay with the girls, Sue."

She pushed him away, hope filling her eyes. "Does that mean you found a job?"

Sam was slow to answer, "Yes and no."

"What does that mean?"

Sam licked his lips. "It seems to me your Thomas Gatlin . . . "

"He is not *my* Thomas Gatlin." Sue held fire in her eyes, "He is *your* cousin."

"Don't remind me. Anyway, Gatlin has done a lot of talking around town. No one would even give me a chance to try a job."

"But you said you had a job?"

"I do."

"Well, what is it, Sam?" Sue looked deep into his eyes.

Sam swallowed, "The salt mines."

"The salt mines in Hutchinson?"

With a deep breath, Sam looked at the ceiling. "I leave tomorrow . . . early. I need to be at the station at five in the morning."

Sue shook her head, "No, Sam, you can't go. Let me find a job. I can go look tomorrow. I'll find something—anything."

Sam was shaking his head. "Sue! Sue! Gatlin has already talked to everyone in Dodge City. That was proved today. Everyone is afraid of him. I don't think there is one single person who will dare to cross him."

"Please," Sue whispered.

"We need the money."

"What about Maggie?" A tear slid from Sue's eye.

"Maggie will be better off with you than she has ever been with me." His voice was breaking, "I don't know about little girls. I don't know how to teach her to grow up the way I know you can, Sue."

Maggie gasped for a breath of air and dropped her forehead against the window sill. Daddy was going to leave her?

Sue shook her head. "Sam, you can't do that to Maggie. It will crush her. You're the only stable thing in her world and you can't take that from her. She already thinks you blame her for her mama's death. If you go off and leave her it will destroy that little girl."

"I don't think she caused her mama's death. I have never thought it was her fault. Why does she think that?" Sam's brow furrowed.

"Maggie heard you say you wished she had gotten you instead of her mama when the neighbor's bull got into the pond. That's why she thinks you blame her."

"Well, I do wish she had gotten me, but it doesn't mean I think it is her fault. Sue, you tell her that so she understands—*please*," Sam pleaded.

"No." Sue looked him in the eye, "You tell her. She needs to hear it from you, not me."

"But I can't say it right, Sue."

"Try, Sam, try." Sue stood firm. She looked at him before she continued, "I'll go call the girls."

Opal scrambled to the ground and sped to Ruby. "Come on, Ruby, Mama's comin'!" She grabbed Ruby and pulled her to her feet.

Ruby glanced at Maggie. Maggie had slid to the ground beside the old water trough. "You thinking again?" Ruby shook her head. "You got to be the thinkingest person I know."

"Well, she'd better do her thinking while heading toward the house," Opal tugged on Ruby's hand.

"I'm coming." Slowly Maggie rose on her shaky legs. Yes, she would come, but she wouldn't stay. Somehow she would go with Daddy. She didn't know how yet, but she was going. She looked up to the God in the stars and then remembered the God that lives in hearts. To both of them she made a promise, "I am going with my daddy."

Walking toward the house, she stopped and threw her hand over the gasp that exploded from her mouth. Daddy didn't blame her for Mama's death. And she hadn't even had to ask him the question. Chills caused her body to shiver. Was that because of the God that lives in hearts?

CHAPTER 8

Gone

"**S**tupid troublemaker," Ruby spat between clenched teeth.

"Well, if you had kept your mouth closed like you were supposed to, they wouldn't have found out. So it is all your fault," Opal shoved her nose in Ruby's face.

"It is not my fault. I didn't even do anything wrong. You did what was wrong, Opal," Ruby glared.

"Oh, yeah? Well, I did it to help everyone. As far as I can tell you just blabbed to get us all in trouble," Opal stuck her tongue out like an exclamation mark.

"I didn't blab. Mama asked me if I was eavesdropping and I couldn't lie to her," Ruby spread her hands.

"Well, you could have just said no. You didn't have to say, 'No, ma'am, that wasn't me on the water trough under the window,'" Opal mimicked.

"Girls! That's enough. There is to be no more discussing. Get your nighties on and get yourselves in bed," Sue dropped the quilt door back into place.

Through the silence that settled in the room, Maggie listened to Sue's footsteps cross the wood floor. She peeled her overalls off, dropped them to the floor, and slid her gown over her head. She waited for Opal and Ruby to crawl across the bed before she climbed in beside them.

When they were settled Ruby whispered to Maggie, "So, how do you like Opal Trouble?"

"Ruby, I'm warning you right now to shut up!" Opal hissed.

"Well, Opal, you got us into a whole big bunch of trouble and I don't like it," Ruby sniffed.

"You're the one who told on us. Now we got double chores for a week."

Maggie swallowed as she heard footsteps again. "I think you both better hush it up before your mama gets here."

Both sisters squeezed their eyes shut and froze into position. Ruby faked a quiet snore, Opal jabbed her in the side, and Maggie stifled a giggle.

The sound of footsteps paused outside the girls' room, then faded away. The girls all breathed a sigh of relief.

"Whew, that was close. Thanks for the warning, Maggie," Opal whispered.

"Sure."

"She just didn't want any more Opal Trouble," Ruby scowled in the darkness.

"Ruby . . . " Opal began.

But Maggie had had enough. "Both of you hush it up and get to sleep before I go get your mama. Ruby, roll over and face the wall. Opal, turn toward me but don't breath on me. I don't like it," Maggie ordered.

Opal gasped, "Some fun a big sister is."

"Good night, Opal." Maggie closed her eyes, "Good night, Ruby."

"Night, Maggie," Ruby sighed. "I like having a bigger sister than you, Opal. She can tell you what to do."

"Ruby, you are going to get it," hissed Opal.

"Opal!" Maggie's voice carried enough warning that both sisters gave up the fight. Thankful the truce brought peace to the bedroom, Maggie lay awake and waited. She could almost feel the tension easing from the girls as they drifted into sleep. The wind outside whined through the fence and rustled the trees. Maggie could hear the clock over the table ticking. Daddy and Sue were in their own room now. She had listened for their door to close. Still she waited. Her eyes grew heavy. She badly needed to move just to stay awake, but she didn't dare to even twitch. The girls must be sleeping soundly before she made her move. An owl hooted in the distance. Finally she heard the familiar snoring she had been waiting for. Daddy was asleep.

Maggie slipped out of bed. She was careful not to get the covers tangled in her feet this time and to stay far away from the firewood that held the bed in place. Crawling over to her carpetbag, gently she peeled her gown off and groped for her overalls. Usually she shook them before she put them on—in case there were any bugs in them—but she didn't dare do that now. When she had the overalls in place she stood up and studied the room in the moonlight.

Most everything was still in her carpetbag since she hadn't yet taken the drawer the girls had cleared out for her. Her brush lay just under the edge of the bed. She tiptoed over, knelt to the floor, and reached for it. Bumping her head on the hunk of firewood, she bit her tongue to keep from yelping.

Ruby rolled over and flopped her arm over Opal. Maggie froze as Opal groaned and muttered for Ruby to quit it. Slowly Maggie took the corners of her pillow in the tips of her fingers and eased it from beneath Opal's head. Then she backed away from the bed and ducked under the quilted door. She leaned against the wall and sighed with relief. In time with the ticking of the clock Maggie padded step by step across the cool wooden floor to the outside door, hoping it wouldn't creak when she opened it. "One, two, three," she mouthed the numbers as she counted. On three she closed her eyes and pulled open the door just wide enough to slip through. It clicked closed, but to her it sounded like a slam.

Already Maggie loved the screened porch. The wind swept through and seemed to brush cobwebs away, leaving fresh hope behind. Maggie breathed deeply. She sank to the porch floor and leaned against the outside of the house. It was okay to sleep now because when Daddy stepped through the door early in the morning it would wake her up—which was what she wanted. Daddy had told her goodbye last night, saying it was better that way. He didn't want to wake her up so early. Well, he didn't want to take her with him either, but Maggie was sure she could convince him.

She sat awake and in her head she listed all the things she would say to him. She wouldn't be a burden—no, she'd be a help. The night owl called and Maggie snuggled close to her pillow. She lay her head in the softness and edged down the wall to curl in a ball around the pillow. Her breathing steadied and her dreams raced. The moon rose to take center stage,

danced among the empty clouds, and bowed at the end of its performance. The sun would soon take the moon's place.

In hours that seemed minutes, the door swung open and Maggie heard voices. "Take care, Sue. It'll be a month at least before I can make it back—maybe more. Use the money I left for you. I know it's not much, but I'll send more as soon as I get a paycheck. In the meantime you can sell milk. Lulubelle's a good ol' milk cow. If you need to, you can sell her. I'd like you to try to keep the horses, but if worse comes to worse you can sell them, too. Then there's the wagon. Sue, I trust you to do what needs to be done. I know this is a rough situation, but the good Lord will see us through. I know he will."

Maggie peeked under her eyelids. Sue just nodded. Maggie watched as Daddy pulled Sue into his arms and talked softly to her. "I am sorry to have to leave you and the girls, but you know it's the only job I'm going to get."

Maggie closed her eyes so she wouldn't hear. It didn't work.

"Sue, I love you," Maggie heard Daddy whisper.

Maggie's heart burst. Why did she have to hear that? She wasn't even trying to eavesdrop this time. She snapped her eyes open and was ready to shout when Daddy kissed Sue right on the lips. Maggie gasped. Then she began to sweat as both pairs of eyes dropped to her.

"Maggie!" It wasn't a question. It was a demand. Shakily Maggie rose to her feet. "I'm waiting," Daddy cleared his throat.

Maggie kicked at the floor. She threw back her head with determination and blurted out, "Daddy, I'm going with you." Daddy's face drained. Maggie watched his jaw muscles tighten as he clenched and unclenched his teeth. "Daddy, I won't be in the way, I promise. I could cook and clean for you and wash your clothes like I did before." Her words tumbled over each other. Daddy shook his head.

"Yes, I could. I'm a good worker. You told Sue that last night."

"No," Daddy whispered. "Honey, no."

"Yes!"

"No." Daddy took a quick step and knelt beside Maggie. "I can't take you to the salt mines. It isn't any place for a little girl."

"I can cut my hair some more and in my overalls I kind of look like a boy anyway. Maybe I could even work in the salt mines, too." Maggie begged.

Daddy shook his head, "No, Maggie."

"Please, Daddy."

"No, Maggie. You are going to stay here with Sue. She is going to take care of you and she's going to do it better than I ever have," Daddy held Maggie at arm's length.

"But I don't want to stay with Sue. I want to be with you, Daddy. I want to go wherever you go. I want to be with you," Maggie's eyes flooded with tears.

"No. This time you can't be with me. You have to stay with Sue," Daddy's eyes began to swim.

"Please, Daddy, please take me with you," Maggie pleaded. Daddy couldn't talk; he just shook his head no. Maggie flung herself into his arms, "Please, please, please!"

Daddy held her tight and whispered, "I love you, Maggie."

"Then you'll take me?"

"Maggie, I can't." He pried her arms from around his neck and looked into her eyes. He shook his head, "No, honey."

"Please?" she whispered.

Daddy shook his head and stood to his feet. "I've gotta go. I can't miss that train. There won't be another one for a week." Daddy paused, "Maggie, be a big girl and help Sue."

Maggie looked to Sue. She was squeezing her stomach and silent tears were streaming down her face. "She doesn't need me Daddy. You do. That's what you always tell me."

"No." Daddy turned, picked up his bag, put on his hat, opened the porch door and stepped out.

Maggie felt like he was stepping out of her life. She grabbed her pillow and carpetbag, stumbled through the screen door, and down the steps. The door slammed. She ran after him, crying, "Wait, Daddy. Don't leave me."

Daddy strode to the gate and hopped over. He didn't look back.

Maggie ran after him, "Wait, Daddy. Wait for me." She dropped all her possessions at the gate and began fumbling with the old latch. Tears blurred her eyes and she couldn't see to open the gate. Sobbing, she sank to the ground. She couldn't catch her daddy now even if she climbed the fence and left all her stuff. Daddy was gone. Her whole body shook.

From behind Maggie, Sue sat down on the dusty path and wrapped her arms around the sobbing girl. Together they rocked and cried. No words were spoken. Through the crisp morning air the whistle of the train sounded the time. Five a.m. Daddy was gone.

CHAPTER 9

Mustard Seeds

The days felt like they must be fifty hours long. If it hadn't been for Opal and Ruby, Maggie knew they'd have felt even longer as they dragged by. It was different having sisters. They offered a companionship she'd never had before. She wasn't sure just what to do with it, but she really was beginning to like it.

Beside the clock over the table was a railroad calendar. Maggie thought it was fitting to have it in the boxcar house. Quietly she crossed to the calendar. After making sure no one was in the room, she took hold of the pencil that was tied to a string and nailed to the wall. Very faintly she marked the day with a small dot. Today was Sunday. She'd been in this new family for one whole week now.

"So that's who's been writing on my calendar," Sue's voice came from behind her and Maggie froze. "I noticed it yesterday and wondered if it was you, Maggie."

Maggie swallowed and turned around. "I'm sorry. I was trying to do it really soft so no one could tell but me." She dropped her eyes to the floor and whispered, "I'll erase them."

"No," Sue stepped beside Maggie and laid her arms on her shoulders. "I rather like the idea of marking off the days so we know when it's about time for your daddy to come home. I think it would be better though if you would put a big "X" across the whole calendar square so it would be easier to see." Sue took her finger and made an "X" in the air.

"You do?" Maggie asked in wonder.

"You bet I do. Why don't you take a minute right now and do that," Sue smiled.

"Thank you," Maggie turned to the wall and boldly remarked the calendar.

"You better hurry it up, Ruby," Opal called over her shoulder as she pushed through the quilt door. "We're ready to load up for church and you're gonna get yourself left."

"Opal," Sue stood with her hands on her hips. "You know we aren't going to go off and leave your sister."

"Yeah, but she doesn't know it and I can't get her to hurry up. She doesn't even have her dress on yet," Opal said.

"I don't have it on because Opal hid it," Ruby whined.

"Opal?" Sue questioned.

"I didn't hide it. I just put it up on the nail on the wall. I did it to help her so it wouldn't be all wrinkled for church," Opal grinned.

"It didn't help me," Ruby complained. "It didn't help me because you stuck it behind everything of yours!"

"Opal, you get in there right now and get if for your sister. Then you tell her you are sorry. We are already running late. Now go help her!"

By the time they pulled the wagon into the church yard they were really late. It seemed everything that *could* go wrong *had* gone wrong. Lulubelle hadn't wanted to hold still for milking and Maggie hadn't had the same strong persuasive touch like Daddy had. Hitching the wagon took twice as long for Sue and Maggie to do together as it did for Daddy to do alone. Then there was the episode of Ruby's hidden dress. Opal would be doing the dishes alone for the rest of the week.

Maggie jumped from the wagon, smoothed her dress, and smiled. She still loved the pink rosebuds and it made Mama feel close. The dress fit much better since Sue had fixed it. She swung a full circle and watched the skirt of her dress fly. Sue had given Maggie a pink bow for the hair she had pulled to the side. Maggie couldn't remember ever wearing a bow in her hair before and she felt pretty. She thought about looking for that Mrs. Crenshaw woman and watching her notice how nice the dress looked and how nice she looked in it.

"Wow, Maggie. Your dress really swings," Ruby giggled.

"Come on, girls. Let's go in. We're late, so be very quiet," Sue warned.

The congregation was singing their last hymn as Sue and the girls pushed through the door. The only empty pew was about three from the front. As they passed each row, the people stopped singing and stared. By the time they got to their pew even the people in front were turning around to watch them. Maggie felt very uncomfortable. If that's the way they looked at late people, she'd rather not even come at all if they were going to be late again. She did find that Mrs. Crenshaw woman, though. Maggie eyed her and watched as her mouth dropped open letting a sour note soar. Ruby giggled and Opal slapped her hand over her sister's mouth. Maggie squeezed between the two girls and Sue mouthed, "Thank you."

Maggie tried to listen to the preacher, but she began to feel nervous as people twisted and turned in their pews to peek at them. Something was wrong. They didn't do that last Sunday. Her mind began to wander and her eyes began to rove. Maybe the squirrel would visit church again this Sunday. Finally, Pastor Olson was done and the last amen was said, but the congregation didn't head for the door. Instead they began to crowd around Sue and the girls.

It was Mrs. Crenshaw who pushed through the crowd and blurted out the question that apparently everyone wanted to ask. "So that new husband of yours jumped the first train out of town and left you saddled with the kid?" Her nose was within inches of Sue's face. "I kind of thought something like that. I sure wish you would have confided in me before this awful tragedy happened." She turned to Maggie, "What are you going to do with her anyway?" She reached over and lifted Maggie's chin to look closely, "You have good teeth!"

Maggie clamped her mouth closed and yanked away from the hateful woman. With her hands on her hips she stamped her feet and shouted, "My daddy didn't hop a train and leave me. He's coming back. He's coming back at the end of the month!"

Quickly, Sue squeezed between the two, "Mrs. Crenshaw! That is enough. My husband did not hop a train and leave us. He went to Hutchinson to work in the salt mines—since no one here was brave enough to stand against Thomas Gatlin and give him a job!"

"Oh. Well, I certainly hope you are right and that he is coming back. It would be awful for you if he doesn't." Mrs. Crenshaw scanned the thinning crowd. "If he doesn't though, I think you could probably send that girl of his out to work. At least it would help ends meet."

"If he doesn't come back, Mrs. Crenshaw, I will not send his little girl out to work. I will keep her and raise her as mine, same as Opal and Ruby," Sue reached behind her and took hold of Maggie's hand.

"Suit yourself. If you want to keep that little ragamuffin spitfire you go right ahead," Mrs. Crenshaw threw her shoulders back and stuck her nose in the air.

A tall, well-dressed man stepped up to Sue. Gently, he reached down and took her hand, glanced at her empty ring finger, then looked into her eyes, "As I said before, no ring, no commitment, and I would say most likely no marriage. My offer still stands. Marry me. I would even take the little ragamuffin spitfire."

Sue dropped Maggie's hand and swung. A gasp spread among the remaining congregation as the slap echoed about the walls of the old church.

From the front steps Pastor Olson stepped back inside, "Everything all right in here?"

"Just fine, Pastor. Thank you for the wonderful sermon about how God's people should treat God's people. I'd love for you to preach it again sometime." Sue grabbed Maggie's hand, "Come on, girls. We've a lot to do today." They walked out of the church and didn't look back.

"Of all the nerve!" Maggie didn't see the speaker, but she knew it was that Mrs. Crenshaw woman.

On the ride home Sue didn't talk. Maggie dared to whisper only one question, "Who was that man your mama slapped?"

"Mr. Thomas Gatlin," Opal mouthed the name.

Maggie nodded, but no one spoke the rest of the way home. When they drove into their yard Sue broke the silence, "Opal and Ruby, go on in and set the table. Maggie, come with me and we'll unhitch the horses."

Ruby and Opal dropped from the wagon. Sue didn't even wait until they were inside. She flicked the reins, and Ben and Maude headed for the lean-to shed. They began unhooking the horses in silence. Finally, Maggie said, "I don't want to go back to that church."

"I don't blame you, Maggie, but we will go back there next Sunday, on time, with our heads held high."

"Why?" Maggie wanted to know.

"Because we have nothing to be ashamed of and because that is what God tells us to do." Sue picked up the curry comb and began brushing Ben, "God knows it is good for us to get together with his people and to learn about him."

Maggie thought for a moment, "It doesn't feel like they are God's people to me."

Sue laughed, "I doubt they are all God's people."

"But they go to church. Isn't that supposed to make them God's people?"

Sue stopped brushing Ben and watched Maggie over the back of the horse. "Well, it should help them know if they are God's people. You see, Maggie, almost everyone knows there is a God somewhere out in the wild blue yonder, but that doesn't make them one of God's people. Jesus gave us a short story in his word that helps to explain it. In Matthew he says the kingdom of heaven is like a grain of mustard seed. It is one of the tiniest seeds, and yet when it is planted, it grows into one of the strongest herb trees there is. In fact it gets so big birds come and make their nests in it."

Maggie furrowed her brow, "I don't understand."

Sue smiled, "Knowing God exists somewhere is like having a mustard seed in your hand. If you keep it in your hand all your life, will it ever grow?"

Maggie shook her head, "You would have to plant it and water it to get it to grow."

"Yes, ma'am, you would. If you know there is a God, it is just like holding the mustard seed in your hand. When Jesus is in your heart, that seed is planted and you will start to grow in the Lord Jesus. You will become a bigger and stronger person. In time, you will be able to offer a shelter in the time of storm to other people, Maggie, just as the mustard seed offers shelter to the birds. I am afraid many of the people in our church are keeping the seed in their hand and it isn't planted in their hearts."

Maggie asked, "I tried to ask him into my heart, but I didn't know for sure how to do it. How do you get him in there?"

"It's easy, Maggie. You ask him. You ask him to forgive your sins and come into your heart." Sue motioned to a bale of hay, "If you would like to pray and ask Jesus to come into your heart, we could do it right here."

Maggie studied the bale of hay. She wanted Jesus in her heart, but she wondered if it would really work. It seemed to be working for Sue. She thought of the mustard seed and rolled the idea around in her mind as if it were in the palm of her hand. If she never planted it, the seed would never grow. If she never asked Jesus into her heart, asking him to forgive her sins, he would never be there. Maggie made up her mind. Yes, she wanted Jesus in her heart. Slowly she crossed to the bale and knelt beside Sue, "What do I say?"

"What do you want, Maggie?"

"I want Jesus to forgive me of my sins and to be planted in my heart," Maggie kept her eyes fixed on Sue.

Sue nodded, "Then that is exactly what you tell Jesus."

Maggie swallowed and dropped her head, "Dear God, I got you in my hand because I know you're out there somewhere, but I need you planted in my heart. Would you please come in and forgive me of all my sins? Amen." Maggie looked up at Sue and was surprised to see tears tumbling down her cheeks. "Are you okay?" she asked.

Sue laughed, "It's worth it all!"

Maggie squinted at her. She wasn't sure just what Sue meant by that, but she had a new feeling inside. It was kind of like hopping out of the bathtub after playing in the dirt or sliding into clean sheets on a hot summer night. It was good.

Then Sue hugged her. Sue hugged her—*and it was okay with Maggie!* It was so okay that Maggie began to cry. It had been three years since she'd had a mama kind of hug. It wasn't the same as Mama, but it was okay.

This Stinks!

"**M**aggie, come on down and help me with Lulubelle. This milking is hard work," Opal complained.

"You said you wanted to learn," Ruby reminded her.

Opal made a face at Ruby. Then she twisted her head toward the rafters again. "Please, Maggie?"

Maggie sighed. She scanned the road again. From the rafters she could see far into the distance. No one was coming. By her calculations Daddy should be home soon. Five weeks had passed. Any day now he would be walking down that road. She wanted to be the first to see him.

"Maggie!" Opal danced around.

"Okay, Opal, I'm coming." Maggie swung from a rafter and jumped to the ground, exploding a dust cloud about her.

"Wow!" Opal breathed, "Aren't you ever afraid?"

Maggie giggled, "I can show you how to do that if you want to learn. It's easy."

"That's what you said about milking Lulubelle." Opal squinted at Maggie with apprehension.

"Lulubelle is a bit cantankerous so you just have to out-smart her." Maggie patted the old cow on the rump and spoke softly to her. "Lulubelle, now hold still and let's get this milking done. Then you can go out and munch all day in the pasture."

Together they squatted beside the cow and Maggie began milking. "Now, you give it a try, Opal."

Opal reached for the cow, but Maggie grabbed her hands. "Wait!" Remember, you have to warm your hands first or Lulubelle will throw a hissy fit you'll not soon forget."

Opal rolled her eyes, "It's summer. Just how cold can summer hands be?"

Maggie shrugged, "Go ahead and try it then, but I have seen her kick right through the barn wall."

Opal cupped her hands together and blew into them. Before long she heard the ringing sound of the milk as it hit the inside of the bucket. Opal decided milking Lulubelle wasn't so bad after all. Then they heard a shout.

"Opal, Maggie, look what I found," Ruby yelled. "You've got to come and see!"

"It'll have to wait. While you've been playing we've been doing what we're supposed to do," Opal scolded.

"It won't wait, Opal. It'll get away and I need your help to catch it. Please," Ruby begged.

"You'll have to wait, Ruby."

"What did you find, Ruby?" Maggie set down the pail of milk she had just picked up. She slipped over behind where Ruby lay on the ground peeking under a pile of old wood.

"Oh, Maggie, it's a kitty cat," Ruby kept her eyes on her

new treasure.

"Are you sure?" Maggie was excited. She loved animals of any kind and a kitten would be a dream come true.

"Yep, I'm sure. I can't reach it though. I been trying, but my arm ain't long enough."

"Let me give it a try, Ruby." Maggie knelt down and peeked under the board pile. She whistled. "Looks like a kitten all right. I can see two glowing eyes and a bunch of black fur." Maggie laid down on the ground so she could stretch her arm all the way to where the kitten was. Finally, she felt fur. She yelled, "I got it! I got it!" She clutched the little ball of fur and pulled. The kitten hissed. Still Maggie pulled, "Hey, there's another one." Before she even had the kitten out from under the woodpile she stuck her other arm in to grab the next one. "Here, Ruby, you take this one," Maggie handed over the first and pulled on the next.

"He's beautiful!" Ruby held the kitten high. "What color is yours, Maggie?"

"I think he's black just like yours," Maggie pulled him into the sunlight.

"I'm showing Mama," Ruby started toward the house.

"Mama won't let you keep it," Opal took the bucket of milk.

"You don't know that for a fact, Opal," Ruby stuck her tongue out at her sister and turned toward the house. "Hey, someone's here," she paused.

"Someone's here?" Maggie asked. Before anyone could answer she shouted, "Daddy's home!" She grabbed the kitten and barreled toward the house, taking the steps in a single leap. She flew through both doors letting them slam behind her.

"Good grief, Sue! Has this ragamuffin spitfire no manners

either?"

Maggie froze. It was not Daddy. It was Mrs. Crenshaw. She wanted to turn around and leave as fast as she had come in, but her feet seemed to be stuck to the floor.

"Oh, my word!" Mrs. Crenshaw grabbed her heart, pinched her nose, and backed against the wall. "That ragamuffin spitfire has brought a skunk into your house!"

Ruby tumbled in behind Maggie with her kitten. "Mama, look at our kitties. Can we keep them?" Ruby's eyes sparkled.

"Of course you can't, child," Mrs. Crenshaw barked from the wall. "Those things smell to high heaven and they carry rabies. Sue, you'd better tell them to throw those things out of here!"

Sue paused a moment to look at Mrs. Crenshaw, then crossed over to the two girls, "Maggie, Ruby, those are the cutest little babies. Would you let me hold one?"

"Humph!" Mrs. Crenshaw glared.

"Here, Mama, you can hold mine," Ruby handed her kitty to her mama.

"I'm warning you, Sue, skunks are known to have rabies. I'd take them out and drown them if I were you!" Mrs. Crenshaw stayed plastered against the wall, still pinching her nose.

Mama stroked the little creature, then handed it back to Ruby. "Honey, this baby is so little that he still needs his mama and . . . honey . . . he *is* a skunk."

"He don't smell like a skunk," Ruby's eyes were pleading.

"Not yet, Ruby, but he will. He's a skunk and he will end up smelling like a skunk," Mama explained.

"But he doesn't now," Ruby's bottom lip quivered.

"That's because he's not quite old enough and his scent

glands aren't fully developed yet. In time he will smell just like a skunk."

"Does that mean we can't keep them?" A tear slid over the edge of Ruby's eye and skidded down her cheek.

"I should think not. No one in their right mind would let their child keep one of those. A skunk! My word!" Mrs. Crenshaw threw the stinging words across the room.

"I told you Mama wouldn't let you keep them," Opal bumped through the door and sloshed the pail of milk.

Ruby ignored her sister. "Please?" she whispered.

Mama shook her head, "You girls put them back where you found them and hopefully their mama will take them and care for them again."

"It would be smarter to drown them, Sue," Mrs. Crenshaw warned.

No one paid attention to the visitor. Mama continued, "Go on—both of you. Take them and put them back where you found them," gently she turned the two girls toward the door and gave them a shove.

"Wait," Mrs. Crenshaw called. "I think your new girl needs to hear what I have come to tell you."

"Maggie?" Sue asked.

Mrs. Crenshaw nodded. "It's important, Sue. That's why I came as soon as I found out. The girl needs to hear this."

"What about Opal and Ruby?" Sue questioned. Mrs. Crenshaw shook her head.

Sue licked her lips and swallowed, "Okay. Opal and Ruby, you take these precious little babies and give them back to their mama." Sue picked the little skunk from Maggie's hands and placed it into Opal's. "Now girls, go give them back."

After the door closed behind them, Sue reached for Maggie's hand and took a deep breath. "Mrs. Crenshaw, what is so important that Maggie needs to hear?"

Mrs. Crenshaw pulled out a rolled-up newspaper and whopped it in the palm of her other hand a couple of times. "This. I just got it today and thought you should know first thing." She unrolled the newspaper and spread it on the table. "Read it for yourself."

Maggie felt Sue's hand tremble and squeeze tight. Her other hand slipped over her mouth as she gasped.

"See, I told you that girl needed to know about this," Mrs. Crenshaw's voice was triumphant.

"Mrs. Crenshaw, she didn't need to know about it like this," Sue sank into a chair. Maggie's eyes dropped to the newspaper and soaked in the headline. Her stomach began to churn.

Salt Mines Collapse: Death Toll Rising

"Just what are you going to do with that girl now that her father is dead?" Mrs. Crenshaw pointed her finger. "I told you he would saddle you with that kid of his. Now you're stuck with her unless you decide to send her out to work or . . . I guess there's always the orphanage."

"Mrs. Crenshaw, please! This article doesn't name Sam among the dead. You don't know that he is." Sue's voice rose as it made its way through sobs.

"No? Just read right down here. Better yet, let me read it to you," Mrs. Crenshaw snatched the newspaper from her. " 'Sam Daniels will forever be remembered as a hero. After pulling three of his co-workers from the collapsed chamber he returned for the remaining miner. Only minutes passed before the mine tunnel timbers gave way.' " Mrs. Crenshaw slapped the paper down on the table and looked directly at Sue. "So what does that tell you except this girl's father is dead?"

"They haven't found his body," Sue looked at the floor.

"It happened five days ago. If you haven't heard he's alive, then most likely he's dead."

"My daddy is not dead!" Maggie screamed.

"Well, he isn't here is he?" Mrs. Crenshaw scrunched her face close to Maggie's.

Maggie's heart hurt so badly she wished she could slug this Mrs. Crenshaw woman. But her daddy—who just had to be alive even if he was a whole week overdue—had taught her better than that. She wadded up her fists and glared at the hateful woman. "Do you know what you need to do? You need to plant a mustard seed. I know it isn't planted because there's nothing good growing in your heart."

"Why, you little snip. Sue, you'd better get rid of this mannerless ragamuffin spitfire while you have a chance," Mrs. Crenshaw snapped.

Sue stood, "Mrs. Crenshaw, please leave."

"What?" The woman was shocked.

"Leave."

"Well! I . . . ."

"Leave, Mrs. Crenshaw . . . just *leave.*"

"All right." She started to reach for the paper on the table, but thought better of it. "I will do the Christian thing and at least leave the paper for you. Maybe that will convince you he's not coming back." She turned and walked out the door, flinging her final words over her shoulder. "Just remember that I warned you."

Maggie listened to the steps cross the porch and the slam of the screen door. She was glad Mrs. Crenshaw was gone. She wished the woman had never come. Sue's arms surrounded Maggie as the silence settled. Maggie felt protected on the outside, but her insides felt like a million bombs were exploding.

"Maggie . . . honey . . . this doesn't prove your daddy is dead. Newspapers don't decide, God does," Sue spoke quietly.

"But he's been gone five weeks. He was only supposed to be gone a month," Maggie sobbed.

"It's only a bit longer than he said and his name is not listed among the dead," Sue encouraged.

"But didn't you hear her? She read that the mine caved in on Daddy," Maggie was trembling.

"It still doesn't say he is dead."

"But he's not here," tears tumbled.

"Maggie, no news is good news, and honey, we have God on our side. We can pray." By now Sue was crying, too, but she took Maggie's hand as the young girl prayed.

"Please, oh please, Jesus that lives in my heart, please bring my daddy home," Maggie struggled through sobs.

They cried together and Sue held her tight for a long time. Maggie wondered if she was praying, too, but all she could hear her say was, "Lord . . . oh Lord," again and again and again.

CHAPTER 11

With this Ring

*M*aggie pulled the quilt tightly about her. She wasn't cold because the room was cold. She was cold because a part of her had died. Maybe by morning all of her would be dead and she wouldn't have to hurt anymore. She closed her eyes to sleep, or to die, whichever happened first. Opal and Ruby were still beside her. They had tried so hard to make her feel better when Sue told them Maggie's daddy had been in an accident. Maggie winced when she thought of Ruby's little gasp, "My *new* daddy?"

She really believed Opal and Ruby liked her. It had been kind of nice to have sisters for a while. But what now? Would Sue keep her? Would she put her in an orphanage? Would she send her out to work as Mrs. Crenshaw had suggested? Maggie shook her head to push those thoughts away. Those were things Mrs. Crenshaw would do, but not Sue—*at least she hoped not.* No, Sue was different than Mrs. Crenshaw. Sue was nice and gentle. Never once had she called her a name like Mrs. Crenshaw had done. Sue had offered her hope when Mrs.

Crenshaw had none to give. Sue was a whole lot different than that woman. Maggie was glad Daddy had married her and not someone like Mrs. Crenshaw.

Maggie shivered and again tried to close her eyes. Silence. No, there was something. She strained her ears to listen. It was Sue. Maggie slipped out of bed and peeked out from behind the quilt door. Sue had the rocking chair pulled close to the stove and she had cocooned herself in a blanket. Tears trickled in a steady flow down her cheeks. Maggie knew what Sue was feeling. She knew now—Sue did love Daddy.

Maggie turned and went to her carpetbag. She had finally put most of her things in the dresser drawer, but her most precious possessions were still in the bag. She pulled it to the window, and in the light of the moon, felt for her treasure. Cold metal hit her fingers and she latched onto it, holding it high to the light of the moon. Mama's wedding ring made a perfect frame for the moon. She closed it in the palm of her hand and tiptoed out to stand beside Sue. Maggie took a deep breath, "Sue?"

Startled, Sue turned, "Oh, honey, what are you doing up? You should be sleeping."

"I couldn't sleep."

"I know, I couldn't either," Sue sighed. "You want to sit on my lap?" She spread the blanket wide in invitation.

Maggie nodded and crawled into the opening. Sue wrapped the blanket around both of them and for the first time since Mrs. Crenshaw had left, Maggie felt warm. They sat that way until Maggie broke the silence.

"Sue?"

"Mmm?"

"I need to give this to you," Maggie fished for the ring, her eyes cast toward the floor. "It was my mama's and I heard Daddy say he had looked for it to give to you and he couldn't find it. That's because I had it," she stretched her hand out for Sue to see the ring.

"And what about you, Maggie? Do *you* want me to have this ring?" Sue slipped her hand under Maggie's chin to direct her eyes into her own.

Maggie nodded, "I want you to have it even if my daddy doesn't come back and even if you decide not to keep me."

"Oh, honey, I will always want to keep you," Sue's voice shook. "Maggie, listen to me. I married your daddy because I wanted to, for better or for worse, just like the wedding vows say. Only I was lucky. I didn't just get your daddy, I got you in the bargain. I can't tell you how good God was in giving you both to me at once."

Sue continued, "Maggie, my first husband and I wanted to have a lot of children, but that never happened. Children are one of the best gifts God gives. In fact they are so precious, they are just like jewels. That's why we named one of our daughters Opal and the other Ruby. Their father used to laugh at me because all my children were going to be named after precious stones like pearl, jade and diamond. They weren't going to have some plain name like Sue. They were going to have special names *for special people*." Sue paused, then went on, "Maggie, you are very special and there is no way I would ever, ever give you away."

"I don't feel very special. I just feel like Maggie with nobody," her voice dwindled to a whisper.

"Oh, you are somebody to your daddy, and somebody to

me, and to the girls. And you are somebody to God, Maggie. Look at me," she paused. "What is your real name?"

Maggie shrugged, "My name is just Margaret Daniels."

"It is?"

"Yep," her shoulders sagged.

"Well, would you like a middle name Miss Margaret Daniels?" Sue's eyes twinkled.

"Can you do that?"

"We surely can. Would you like that?"

"Oh, yes. Could I pick one of your jewel names?" Maggie's eyes sparkled.

"Yes, you surely can. Just which one would you like?"

"Can I have Pearl? Pearls are so creamy and white and sometimes they reflect other colors—kind of like pale rainbows in a crystal ball." Maggie studied Sue's face to see if it was really okay.

"Let's try it out." Sue raised her head high as if she were announcing royalty, "Margaret Pearl Daniels. How does *that* sound?"

"It's beautiful. Are you sure it's okay?"

"Yes, Margaret Pearl Daniels, I'm sure. And I am also sure it is late and tomorrow is Sunday." Sue stroked Maggie's hair. "We are going to have a short night and we have got to get to bed."

"Do we have to go to church tomorrow?" Maggie whispered.

"Yes, we do. God's people go to meet with God in his house. He *tells* us to do that, He doesn't ask us to do it. Besides, we are asking miracles of God. If we want him to make those miracles happen, we'd better be doing what he tells us to do," Sue didn't waver.

"Okay." Maggie unwound from the blanket they shared, "Good night."

"Good night, Margaret Pearl. I would be honored to wear your mama's ring, but anytime you want it back, it will be yours. All you need to do is ask." Sue smiled as she slid the ring onto her finger.

Sue was right. It was a short night and the morning was hectic. Maggie found herself sitting in church much too soon. Sue had squeezed Maggie between Opal and herself, and Maggie sure was glad. She felt warm and a little protected between them. Maybe Sue should have squeezed between the girls, however, because Mr. Thomas Gatlin was making his way to her side. He put his arm around Sue and assured her he was very sorry for what had happened at the salt mines and to let her know her job would be waiting for her Monday morning if she would like it back. He stroked her cheek and spoke softly, telling her his offer still stood. Sue dropped her gaze to her hand and rolled the simple golden band. When Mr. Gatlin saw the ring, he removed his arm from around her shoulders and walked to a different pew without taking his eyes off Sue.

Maggie's attention switched back to the people around her. Everyone had looked at them in a funny way when they came into church. They kept saying nice things about how sorry they were to hear the sad news that her daddy was gone. Maggie wished they had been that nice to her the first time she and Daddy came to their church. If someone could have been nice enough to give her daddy a job, he wouldn't have had to go away to find one.

Across the aisle Maggie could see Mrs. Crenshaw staring at them. It made her wonder at what Sue had said about God's

people coming to God's house. Why did people that *weren't* God's people come to God's house? Maybe they wanted to pull the wool over everyone's eyes—even God's. Probably the only one they were really fooling was themselves. Boy, were they going to be surprised when they died! Maggie glanced over at Mrs. Crenshaw and decided she'd better start praying for the woman, because her surprise might not be so very far away and she didn't want even Mrs. Crenshaw to go there.

Pastor Olson's deep voice broke into Maggie's thoughts as he began, "We were all saddened to learn of the tragedy in the Daniel's family. Even though Sam had been a member of our community for only a few short weeks, he was found to be a man of courage and integrity. He was recorded to have given his life saving his fellow workers and that in itself reminds us of our Lord Jesus Christ who said, 'Greater love hath no man than this, that a man lay down his life for his friends.'

"That is exactly what Christ did for you and me. He laid down his life for us so we might live. Sam Daniels patterned his life after his Lord and Savior, Jesus Christ. We should all take his example to heart."

He continued, "Sue, Maggie, Opal, Ruby . . . our hearts are heavy for you. We pray that our Lord will give you the strength to see you through this valley. You have lost a husband and a father that cannot be replaced. It is my prayer that our church family will be what we need to be in the coming days and weeks. Sue, we've all gathered some goods for you. They're in the back of the church. The men will load them in your wagon after the service."

Sue mumbled a thank you through stifled sobs. Maggie dropped her head so no one would see her tears. Opal reached over to grab Maggie's hand and hold it tight. Ruby's bottom lip trembled, "You mean my new daddy is really dead?"

Silence traveled over the congregation until Mrs. Crenshaw shocked everyone as she asked loudly, "Sue, do you mean to tell me you didn't tell that child her new daddy is dead?" The whole church gasped.

Ruby began bawling. Opal was crying, too, and tears were streaming down Maggie's face. Maggie wished she had never heard of that Mrs. Crenshaw woman.

"Sue, you should have told those girls! What were you thinking?" Mrs. Crenshaw blurted.

"Mrs. Crenshaw, please," Sue spoke quietly.

"But they need to know," Mrs. Crenshaw continued. The woman's husband jabbed her in the ribs and warned her under his breath to keep quiet. She glared at him. Her raised eyebrows carried a storm, but she didn't say another word.

Just then Pastor Olson spoke in an awesome voice, "Our Lord God Almighty . . . "

Maggie yanked her eyes from Mrs. Crenshaw to the pastor. He was white as a sheet as he stared at the door. Maggie followed his gaze and gasped. She was *not* seeing things. It was Daddy!

"Daddy!" She jumped to her feet and bolted to the back where Sam Daniels half stood on one crutch. He was unshaven, but that didn't hide the bruises and deep crevices in his face. His clothes were filthy, torn, and bloodstained. One arm hung in a sling and a bandage was wound about his head. With his good hand he held his crutch and what was left of his hat. He looked awful, but to Maggie he looked wonderful and she flew into his arms.

"Daddy! Daddy! They said you were dead, but Sue kept saying no one could know for sure. She said it was up to God, not the newspaper. You aren't dead!"

"No, pumpkin, I'm not dead, but only because of the good Lord. It was close and I kind of think God just told Satan he wasn't going to win this one," Maggie's daddy smiled.

Maggie didn't know when Sue and the girls had joined her, but they were all hugging on her daddy, too. This time she didn't mind sharing him one single bit. She was glad she had a daddy to share.

Pastor Olson shook himself and took control. "As I was saying, our Lord God Almighty is a God of miracles and we have the honor of beholding one of his miracles standing in our midst! Brother Sam Daniels, welcome back to the land of the living. We are glad to have you among us!"

"Pastor, I'm glad to be here. I'm sorry to be such a mess, though," Sam's voice sounded weak.

"I should think. Imagine coming into God's house looking like that!" Mrs. Crenshaw shook her head in disgust.

"Keep your mouth shut!" Mr. Crenshaw exclaimed under his breath.

"Sorry, Pastor Olson, I hope I haven't ruined your sermon," Daddy sank lower on his crutch.

"Sam, I think you have been our sermon today," Pastor Olson smiled. "Let's pray."

When the last amen was said, the crowd swarmed about the Daniels family. Maggie's daddy told his story about how the men he had rescued refused to give up on him. They had worked day and night to find him and the other man, dead or alive. For five long days they dug without stopping. When one man got tired someone else would take his place. Even strangers had taken turns and someone had always been there to offer food and water to the weary workers.

Maggie's daddy told them how in the darkest hour he had clung to the promise that God would never leave him. More than a few tears fell as he shared with the congregation that his co-worker had died in his arms before they had been pulled out of the collapsed mine shaft. Praises rang through the rafters of the small church as Maggie's daddy shared how those men, tired and weary, had stood together to offer thanksgiving to God. Then he told how they had all chipped in to buy him a train ticket home.

Along with sheer happiness, pride welled up in Maggie's heart. It would be reported in the newspapers all across the country that her daddy was a hero! Relief swallowed them when they finally crawled into the wagon and headed for the boxcar home. Maggie's daddy took the long way to avoid Thomas Gatlin's place. He eased under a shade tree, pulled to a stop, and turned to Sue. With his good hand, he fumbled in his pocket and took out a wad of money. "Look, Sue, now we can go and get you a wedding ring."

"Sam, that won't be necessary," Sue displayed her left hand. The gold band glinted in the light.

"Where? How?"

"Maggie," smiled Sue.

"Maggie?" Sam still hadn't a clue as to what had happened.

Maggie poked her head between the two of them and explained, "Daddy, I heard you tell Sue you wanted to give Mama's ring to her, but you couldn't find it. That's because I had it. At first I didn't want her to wear Mama's ring, so I didn't tell anyone I had it."

"Do you care if she has it now?" Maggie's daddy asked.

Maggie shook her head. "Daddy, I think Sue loves you an awful lot. And she cried almost all night last night, and she told me she would keep me even if you never came back, and Daddy, she gave me a precious jewel name because she says I am precious to her," Maggie sniffed as tears rolled down her face.

"What name did she give you?"

"Margaret Pearl Daniels. Isn't it beautiful?" Maggie beamed.

"It sure is, Margaret Pearl," Sam hugged his little girl and winked over the top of her head at Sue.

"Maggie," Sue put her hand on Maggie's shoulder. Maggie looked up in question.

"You know how we talked about names, and how mine is just a regular kind of name, and how I wanted all of my children to have special names?" Sue paused and nibbled on her bottom lip in thought.

"Yes," Maggie nodded.

Sue took a deep breath, glanced at Sam, and continued, "Maggie, I would be honored if you would give me a very precious name."

Maggie tipped her head, "Like Jewel or Diamond?"

"No," Sue hesitated. "One I think is even better."

"What?" Maggie couldn't think of anything better than those names.

Sue's voice quivered, "Mama."

Maggie gulped in disbelief, "You would let me call you Mama?"

"I would be honored, Margaret Pearl," Sue struggled to finish her sentence without crying.

"Mama." Maggie dropped her head, "Dear God that lives in my heart, thank you for bringing my daddy home, and dear God, thank you for giving me another mama. You make me feel pretty special to have both of them because it isn't everybody that gets that. Amen."

"Our God is a God of miracles," Daddy rumbled. "Let's take this family home."

**SANDRA WAGGONER** grew up on a farm in western Kansas. Her playground stretched from the yard, to the fields and out into the pasture. She climbed every tree on the place, but her favorite prairie tree was the windmill. She loved to shinny to the top and feel the wind surge through the blades and pump the water from deep within the ground. It seemed that she was in rhythm with the very heartbeat of the earth. Her early Kansas years are where her stories were born. "I think I have always written," she says. "I still have a poem I penned around third grade. In junior high I wrote while I daydreamed in my classes. In high school I wrote for our school newspaper. I wrote while driving the tractor or the wheat truck as my dad's farmhand. I wrote in college. I wrote. I wrote. I wrote. And I write."

Waggoner loves teaching—whether it is her Sunday School class or her fourth grade elementary school class. "Children keep me young and dreaming," she says. "They are the best audience for my work." Sandra is also a speaker, a pastor's wife, and mother of four children. She and her husband make their home in Amarillo, Texas.

Watch for these future books in the *Gatlin Fields* Series

In the Shadow of the Enemy

When Secrets Come Home

www.sablecreekpress.com